Ellis Peters has gained universal acclaim for her crime novels, and in particular for *The Chronicles of Brother Cadfael*, now into their seventeenth volume.

Funeral of Figaro

Ellis Peters

HEADLINE

ISBN 0 7472 3371 3

Printed and bound in Great Britain by
Collins, Glasgow

HEADLINE BOOK PUBLISHING PLC
Headline House
79 Great Titchfield Street
London W1P 7FN

CHAPTER ONE

IT WAS CURIOUSLY appropriate that he should arrive just in the middle of " Deh vieni non tardar," at the precise spot in the fourth act when he was later to make his exit. The purposeful chaos of a piano rehearsal disguised the significance of the moment, and dulled the impact of his coming into a mere natural quiver of interest and awareness; but afterwards they remembered it as if with a quickened vision, and even believed they had had premonitions of disaster.

Slumped on his back in the front row of the stalls, with his crossed feet on the balustrade of the orchestra pit, Johnny listened with delight to Tonda, and kept his eyes closed to avoid seeing her. It wasn't that she was ugly; far from it, she was thought by some sound critics to be rather like her celebrated countrywoman Gina Lollobrigida. In Susanna's bell skirts and tightly-laced bodices she looked enchanting, but she was rising forty, and she really ought not to come to rehearsals in black ballet tights and thick mohair sweaters. She hadn't acquired the nickname of Tonda for nothing, and the impression of a ball of angora knitting wool transfixed by black plastic needles was overwhelming. But she sounded wonderful, worth every lavish pound he was paying for her three rôles in the season's repertoire.

Some Susannas made " Deh vieni " too arch, some too ethereal, the utterance of a disembodied spirit. Tonda knew better. Her Susanna was a flesh and blood

5

woman and her voice took up the deliberate, maliciously
seductive invitation to love with all the vengeful
subtlety of which the female is capable, tormenting
her listening lover with the certainty that she was not
addressing him, and then gradually in the middle of
her teasing she forgot her grudge, forgot the very face
of the Count, and was indeed singing to Figaro, pouring
out to him all the rapture and excitement of her wedding
night in soft, thrilling, aching cries of passion. And
still the fool didn't realise!

That was what Tonda could do with her voice, make
you believe in the profundities of human love even at
rehearsal, and turn back the convoluted leaves of
comedy one by one to delve into the deepest places of
the heart after Mozart. Provided you didn't look at her
there was no limit to the marvellous potentialities she
could suggest. Johnny kept his eyes closed, even when
by the faint stirring of the air and the fragrance of
muguet he knew that Gisela had slipped round to take
the seat beside him. He turned his face towards her
and smiled blindly, and she touched his hand with one
finger, and they listened together.

Count Almaviva, in grey slacks and a sports shirt,
stood with folded arms in the wings, listening atten-
tively. Cherubino, in toreador pants and one of
Johnny's old sweaters—seemingly sweaters were just
the right size these days if you could get into 'em twice
over—copied his attitude and his gravity, her fair
head tilted, her grey eyes fixed respectfully upon the
singer.

Across the stage from them the Countess, tall and
stately and immaculate in a closely-tailored suit that
made her Scandinavian legs look even longer and more

delectable than usual, divided her critical attention between Tonda and the Count.

He was young for the rôle, a rising star out of Austria, not yet used to being famous. What he had in voice and natural ability he still lacked in experience, and it was no small honour for him to be asked to sing so important a rôle opposite Inga Iversen. She had been at pains to be gracious to him. It was necessary that someone should take him in hand, or the predatory Italian woman would ruin him. And that would be a pity, for he had a fine voice and some acting ability. And such eyes! Blue as gentians, and of a heartrending innocence. Also he was that marvel, a partner tall enough for her. Inga had suffered untold embarrassments at the hands of short, tubby Counts.

In the most remote corner of the orchestra pit Doctor Bartolo and Don Basilio sat cheek by jowl, shirt-sleeved and comfortable, their backs propped solidly against the wooden barrier, their cynical elderly eyes swivelling knowingly from Tonda's rapt face and heaving bosom to Inga's aristocratic calm, behind which the feline claws flexed themselves thoughtfully in secret.

Doctor Bartolo was lean and cadaverous and dignified, and as English as a wet summer, and his name was Max Forrester. Don Basilio was short and rosy, pepper-and-salt haired, and with the Welshman's bold, strongly-marked bones and tough, weathered flesh. He had sung Don Basilio so often in his thirty years on the stage that he sometimes had difficulty in remembering that his name was Ralph Howell. Tenor character parts of any quality are comparatively few and far between, he had taken some pains to corner the best of them as soon as he became resigned to being forty years old.

They were conducting a laconic conversation in an almost soundless, almost motionless style that would have done credit to two old lags under the warder's eye.

"What did I tell you?" said Don Basilio, digging an elbow into his friend's lean ribs. "You're on a loser, boy. Tonda's got him dazzled."

"They're only warming up yet," returned Doctor Bartolo confidently. "Wait until Inga gets to him with the great forgiveness phrase at the end."

"Ah, a couple of bars, man, what's that after a brain-washing like this? Look at him! Ravished to the soul, poor lad! You might as well pay up now, you've said good-bye to that fiver."

"I'll still put my shirt on Inga. Want to raise the stake?"

"Double it," offered Don Basilio promptly, survey-ing the ample charms of the lady who carried his money, and dwelling with professional pleasure on the melting ease with which she turned the lovely high phrase and sank in a series of soft falls, like a dove descending. Backstage half a dozen of Johnny's ship's company were listening to it no less appreciatively, straightening and stilling among the surrealist detail of their half-assembled sets. Perhaps the greatest love song ever written for a woman sank to its close in triumphant stillness, like a folding of wings.

"Mate," said Stoker Bates, scratching thoughtfully at the back of his grizzled neck, "that's a bit of all right, that is. You can have all your *Traviatas* and your 'Oh, my beloved daddies' for one drop o' Mozart."

The dove settled and nestled, soft as down.
"'*Ti vo la fronte incoronar—incoronar di rose.*'"

Old Franz Hassilt at the piano echoed the rounded cadence and drew breath to croak the indignant comment of the missing Figaro, for whom he delighted to do duty; but the interjection was taken clean from his lips by a great voice that spat the " *Perfiaa!* " over their startled heads from the doorway on the right of the stalls.

" 'Traitress! So all the time she meant to betray me!' "

Cherubino flashed round open-mouthed, forgetting the trill she had been about to launch after Figaro's line. Johnny opened his eyes abruptly and came leaping to his feet, Franz whirled on the piano stool, and every head turned expectantly to examine the Leander Theatre's new bass-baritone.

His fame had come before him, and they were curious and wary, for they had to measure their powers side by side with his from now on. It was only by luck Johnny's agent had been able to sign him up at all; after the loss of Raimondo Gatti in the plane crash at Vienna they might well have had to make do with a minor artist and be thankful, but fate in the shape of an army cabal in Latin America had effectively cancelled a prior engagement, and presented them with the chance of a lifetime to get Marc Chatrier, and Jimmy Clash had jumped at it. Johnny could stand the racket; grand opera was the one undertaking on which Johnny had ever managed to lose money, and he needed it to ease his tax position, so he said. One of the biggest sums even he had ever paid out was very well spent on the greatest living Figaro.

And there he was, just within the doorway, looking them over with calm, quizzical eyes and visibly selecting Johnny from among them as the man to be reckoned with. Johnny came bounding like a Saint Bernard dog, shoving out a brown fist and beaming.

"Mr. Chatrier, this is wonderful! We didn't expect you to show up this morning, after your journey. I'm sorry I couldn't meet you myself at the airport last night, but I hope Mr. Clash looked after you properly."

Jimmy always looked faintly bewildered when he was referred to as Mr. Clash. He was so used to being Number One or Jimmy the One that the rare occasions when he got his proper name, for the benefit of newcomers who couldn't yet be expected to understand the peculiarities of the Leander Theatre, jolted him like being suddenly confronted with a distorting mirror. He beamed back happily at his employer and friend, proud of his errand and of the acquisition he had brought them.

"Are you comfortable at the Grand Eden? It's a longish drive out here, but there'll be a car at your disposal for the season."

"All your arrangements worked admirably," said Marc Chatrier in his black velvet voice, "and the hotel seems excellent."

They were much of an age, and matched each other in vigour and glow so evenly that the meeting of their hands should have started a flurry of sparks. Johnny was brown and bright, with thick russet hair greying at the temples, and an uneven, mobile, responsive face. Chatrier was black-haired and black-eyed and self-contained, with the quirk of a slightly quizzical smile never far from his lips. The experienced face was a little lined, the dark eyes a little world-weary, but he knew how to wear even these ominous signs as added graces.

"What's the betting," murmured Ralph Howell, eyeing this formidable new competition, "the girls don't switch their attentions?"

Doctor Bartolo considered the possibility thoughtfully for a moment, and shook his head resolutely. "No. Youth has it. They'll stick to the coming lad. This one's been. He's on his way back."

"Come and meet everyone." Johnny had an arm lightly about his new Figaro's shoulders, and a hand outstretched for Franz Hassilt. "You must know our musical director—everyone knows Franz. Without him we could never have made our reputation in such a short time. Without me, of course, he'd have managed it in half the time. We fight a lot, but he always wins."

The old man, wonderful hair erected like a blazing silver aureole, gaudy shirt a dazzle of greens and reds, peered narrowly from the intelligent eyes that could be so gentle and so fierce, and said sharply: "Johnny is a humbug. He treats opera like a toy, but Johnny loves his toys. Nobody crosses Johnny in his play." He blinked up at the tall man whose hand he held, and said with satisfaction: "Mr. Chatrier, at last I get a Figaro who menaces instead of blustering. Now we show them a production as it should be."

"We can at least try," agreed Marc Chatrier gravely.

"And here's our Countess, Miss Iversen. Miss Gennoni, your Susanna. And Cherubino—my daughter Hero."

"Enchanted!" said Marc Chatrier, dividing the

small gallantries of glance and smile and caressing voice between the three of them. Not quite evenly.

A brittle Norwegian icicle whom he already knew, a plump Italian kitten, and a boy-girl in trousers and sweater. Honey-fair, grey-eyed. The girl held his eyes longest. So millionaire Johnny Truscott had a daughter, had he? Could she really sing, or was the impresario only a fond and foolish father who thought she could? Well, he could afford to pay for both their fancies.

Hero said: " Hallo! " airily, like a blunt but assured boy, the approximate blend of gaucherie and self-confidence turned out by the English public school.

" You can see she's well into the skin of the part," said Johnny, grinning. " Dress her up in a party frock now and take her out, and you're liable to get run in. She swaggers about as if she had riding-boots on under her skirt — like Octavian in the third act of *Rosenkavalier*."

" It's your own fault," said Hero, grinning back. " You shouldn't have given me such a silly name if you didn't want me to get complexes. I'm going to sing all the transvestist parts, Mr. Chatrier. Ending up with Octavian."

" I imagine the process will take a few years," he said, and smiled fully for the first time.

" I imagine it will. But Cherubino's a good beginning."

" And here's Max Forrester," said Johnny, " our Bartolo. And Ralph Howell, who sings Basilio."

The alert black eyes assessed, pondered, discarded. Forrester was a good second-rate artist of the kind England bred in considerable numbers, Howell one of the perennial Welsh tenors who end up entertaining at smoking concerts.

"And the Count—you haven't met Hans Selverer?" Johnny was proud of him. "Believe me, he's going to make the critics sit up when we open with this production."

The young man wasn't yet used to being famous, he blushed when he was praised. At first glance a big, good-looking simpleton; at second glance a stubborn, detached intelligence standing off the newcomer and measuring him as exactly as he was himself being measured.

"Selverer!" Chatrier was smiling; the quality of the smile was still ambivalent, perhaps it always would be. "I recall that name." Several eyebrows rose at that; the past year had seen a great deal of newsprint lavished on the boy's achievements. "No, no," said Chatrier easily, "I mean from some years ago, when you can have been no more than a child. Was your father also a musician?"

"A conductor," said Hans, a little grave and constrained as always when too much attention began to concentrate at close quarters on his person or his affairs.

"Yes—that's it! I believe I met him once in Vienna, just before the war."

"It could be so," said the young man, but without volunteering more.

"I lost sight of him after that. Is he still conducting?"

"He is dead. He died during the war."

"Ah, I'm sorry! A great pity!"

"And Marcellina—you must meet our Marcellina," said Johnny, delicately snapping off this tightening thread of conversation before it could stretch too cruelly thin. " Where *is* Gisela? She was with me only a few minutes ago."

" I'm here," said Gisela's serene voice, and she came out of the shadows under the circle stalls. So that was what she'd been up to, restoring her make-up for the occasion. A new, firm bow to her mouth, and every hair in place. A faint, astonished sting of jealousy pricked Johnny's heart. Since when had she gone to the trouble to put on a new face for any man? She never bothered for him.

" Marc Chatrier—Gisela Salberg. Gisela is our Marcellina, and much more than that. I don't know what we should do without her."

She stepped into the light, and he saw her fully. A slender woman of middle height, with a great sheaf of black hair coiled on her neck, and the pale oval face that went with such hair, magnolia-skinned and still, only the large dark eyes and the mobile lips quick with suggestions of humour and feeling. Forty-five, perhaps. Very elegant. She looked up at him steadily, the social smile just curving her lips. A nerve quivered in her cheek. Marc Chatrier smiled at her from under half-lowered lids, hooding the smile from the light and the onlookers, but not from her.

" We're very fortunate to have so notable a Figaro," said Gisela in her clear, cool voice. " I hope we shall be able to work well together, Mr. Chatrier."

God, thought Johnny, he must have made an impression. When did she ever go so far upstage for me?

" I'm sure we shall, Miss Salberg, I'm sure we shall. After such a charming welcome," said Chatrier, smiling at her, his voice heavy and smooth as cream, " I feel that you and I are old friends already."

" But the crew don't like him," said Johnny, raking with worried fingers through his erected hair, and slamming a drawer of his desk shut on the rest of the cares of the day.

" Who says they don't ? " objected Gisela mildly from her perch on the end of the desk.

" No one says, they don't have to say. I know that gang too well to need any telling. You'd think they had an instinct about him. And yet he took them in his stride, you saw that, never batted an eyelid. And you must admit they can be disconcerting on first acquaintance. And he's all right at rehearsals, isn't he ? " Chatrier had been working with the cast for ten days now, if there was anything to be discovered against him it should have begun to show at the rubbed edges. " Franz seems to be thoroughly happy about him."

" With reason. He's a splendid artist. He isn't too easy to work with, perhaps, but it's because he's a perfectionist. I know he's lavish with advice and suggestions, I know he can be exacting. But he's nearly always right. He wouldn't have Franz's goodwill if he wasn't. What are you worrying about ? Rehearsals have gone well, and you're going to have a very fine production."

" Yes," he admitted more cheerfully, " yes, I think so. But I wish he wouldn't treat young Hans as a raw recruit——and slow on the uptake at that ! The boy's as fine in his way as Chatrier——"

" That could be the trouble," said Gisela, with a wry smile.

"Yes, I suppose it could." He brightened; jealousy was a very human reaction from a man at the peak of his career towards a youngster who had soared to the front rank in no more than three seasons, and had at least twenty-five years of fame before him with any luck. "And I hand it to the kid, he's as obstinately good-tempered as a saint. And yet there's this odd way the boys draw in their horns whenever Chatrier comes by. They've been with me a long time, they've developed a kind of feeling for when things are going right and when they're off the rails. And they don't like him. Sam used to smell bad weather before it came, and now I see him sniffing the air just the same way. They go about quietly, not saying anything, just watching. Damn it, sometimes I think they're uncanny myself."

He didn't mean it, he was only being faintly peevish after a long, tiring day. To him there was nothing at all to set his ship's company apart from ordinary people, except the mutilations and disabilities they had suffered under his leadership during the war, and by those he was bound to every one of them for life. The theatre was full of his staunch pensioners, though he would have objected strongly to that word. He paid them a good wage, and they did what they could in return for it, and sometimes Johnny was afraid that left him a long way in their debt.

It was because of them rather than as an expression of his own nostalgia that he had given his theatre its name; so many of the survivors of *Hellespont's* crew shifted its scenery and minded its stage-door and stoked its furnaces that it could have no other name but one closely recalling their old ship. And they had adopted it with all the enthusiasm they had given to the ship, and ran it like one of their old secretive, ramshackle, effective naval operations.

Probably no one now even remembered what discerning genius at Admiralty had recognised in Johnny Truscott, aged twenty-three and in his first command, a born buccaneer, and seconded him and his cockleshell to secret duties; but whoever he was, he had done well by England and by countless refugees and prisoners of war in Europe, and very well, in the long run, by Johnny himself. They'd taught him how to smuggle, how to infiltrate through even the strict and wary controls of wartime, how to ferry saboteurs and information into occupied territory, and wanted persons and more information out again; and Johnny had found his métier and bettered the instruction, until not even his instructors knew the half of what he was up to.

If his raids were also highly profitable to himself, at least England had no cause to complain of any losses on him. And was it his fault if he couldn't settle down to a quiet, law-abiding life after the war, and went on with his old business? Not always to England's satisfaction then, it must be admitted; as, for instance, the Israel period. By then he'd had three ships, all busy running illegal immigrants. Now he had ten, and they seldom smuggled anything more reprehensible than wine and brandy.

The spice had departed to some extent with the need; he was so rich that there was no point in exerting himself to grow even richer. Johnny himself fondly imagined that he was settling down and becoming middle-aged and respectable, whereas the truth was that he was as restless and venturesome at forty-five as he'd been at twenty-five. And as attractive, thought Gisela,

looking down at the tangled brown shock-head he
nursed in his hands, and the blunt, bold, sunburned
face of an experienced and formidable but still ardent
boy. Hopeful of all things, curious about all things.
All he'd done was to pour his surplus energy into a new
channel. He had approached grand opera dubiously,
for Hero's sake, but he had fallen for it with one of the
biggest bangs in history, and no one had been more
surprised than he.

"And you're unsettled, too," said Johnny unexpectedly, turning his head abruptly and catching her
eyes thus brooding upon him. "I can feel it. It's all
since he came."

"No," she denied half-heartedly.

"Yes, I always know by the look on your face when
you start looking back and remembering."

"Don't be silly, what earthly difference could he
make to me? I do look back sometimes, but haven't
I good reason?"

"Not any more. You should have forgotten all that
by now." Johnny rose and stretched himself. "Come
on, I must drive you home."

She had a service flat in a new block no great distance
from his house at Richmond, and they made their
journeys to and from the theatre companionably
together.

"*Cosi* went well to-night," said Johnny, reaching
his hat down from the peg behind the door; and the
warmth of delight came back lightly into his voice as
he returned to his passion.

"Yes, very well."

"Franz is at the top of his powers. Seventy-five
years young." He took her arm, hugging it to his side

in a convulsion of pleasure at the perfection of his toy, and her shared delight in it. " Three days to the première of *Figaro*. It *is* going to be good, isn't it? "

" Of course, you know it is."

He didn't really need her reassurance, he was only exulting and inviting her to exult with him. As she'd been doing now for twenty years, ever since he'd dropped a tree across the road, and snatched her out of the car that was taking her to the clearance camp for Jewish women, en route for Ravensbruck. She had been one of very many who owed their lives and liberty to Johnny and his contacts, but to her he had come as a restoration of man to grace, a kind of miracle when she had felt herself discarded, forsaken and utterly without faith. What use was it for him to tell her she should forget? To forget the betrayal would have been to lose the revelation of faith regained. Gisela preferred to keep both.

Or perhaps it was all so much simpler than that. Perhaps she had merely clung to him ever afterwards for the most female of all reasons, because she loved him. And his wife, and his child, and his shipmates, and all the waifs and strays he accumulated around him, and every little dog that had the sound judgment to stop and speak to him in the street.

She caught one last glimpse of Eileen's photograph in its silver frame on the desk, before Johnny switched off the light and closed the door. Grey-eyed and black-lashed and honey-fair, like her daughter; and fifteen years dead. Poor Johnny! The bad partners never die young.

They went down the carpeted stairs together, Johnny's hand at her elbow. The lavish, rambling spaces of the theatre were growing quiet, the lights going out in the corridors. Glasses clinked softly to a murmur of tired, contented voices in the circle bar, and Dolly Glazier called a good night to them as they passed. Below in the foyer old Sam Priddy rolled across the dim, splendid purple and gold carpeting on his two odd legs, both shortened after the explosion in the engine-room, but shortened unevenly so that he went always with a heavy list to port. He opened the door for them, and roared: " Hey, Codger! " over his shoulder; and in a moment Codger Bayliss came running eagerly with his knitting rolled up under his arm, the steel needles clacking to his ungainly gallop.

Johnny was never allowed to get into a car without Codger being present to open the door for him and shut it with a conscientious slam. If Johnny ever fell out of a car in motion, it wasn't going to be because Codger hadn't closed the door properly.

" You want to watch out to-night," said Sam, eyeing with a frown the overcoat he did not consider warm enough for November. " There's a thin wind come up. Shouldn't wonder it'll drop in the small hours and there'll be frost."

" I'll be careful, grandma. Went well to-night, Sam. How did you like Inga's Fiordiligi? "

There had been a time when Gisela had wondered if Sam really liked opera, or whether it was only a reflected glow from Johnny's pleasure that made him burn bright when it was mentioned. Now she accepted his passion, and did not question its nature.

" Smashing, skipper! " Sam whistled a line of the lady's melting and agitated self-reproaches; he knew whole operas by heart.

And there was the Bentley, just drawing up smartly at the foot of the steps, the wheel almost invisible within Tom Connard's enormous, gentle hands. Codger reached for the handle of the door and held it open for them.

Since his disaster Codger never aged, never worried; a kind of dim understanding of essential things like daylight and warmth and love moved behind the mute and arrested face, and sometimes there was a faint tremor of wonder and disquiet, as though recollection stirred for a second; but never for longer. The large, calm, chiselled features, lit by those big, devoted eyes, had a beauty he had certainly never possessed while the mind behind them had troubled and racked him.

Johnny smiled at him and twitched at the dangling end of green wool, but only to tease him, not hard enough to drag a stitch from the needle.

" Thanks, Codger! Sorry I kept you waiting. Now you get Dolly to pack up quickly, and I'll send the car back for you."

Codger lived with Sam, and Dolly had a flat in the same house, and looked after them both. The house belonged to Johnny, and the rent they paid for it was a sop to their independence.

Johnny looked back as they drew away, to see the lighted façade of his darling recede and dwindle until he lost it at the first corner. The Leander Theatre. Fifth winter season. Within easy reach of London by bus or underground. The only enterprise on which Johnny Truscott lost money regularly and heavily. But it was worth ten times his losses to him.

" Just imagine," said Johnny, sliding down on to the small of his back with a deep sigh of content, " if there'd been no Mozart! What on earth would it have been like, trying to live without him?"

Franz Hassilt rapped irritably for the tenth time, gathered the phlegmatic attention of his orchestra with snapping fingers, and ordered: "Gentlemen, gentlemen, once more! We are tired, I know, but once more. From: '*Cognoscite, Signor Figaro, questo foglio . . .*'"

The four people on the stage drew breath wearily, for he had worked them hard. Susanna and the Countess hovered uneasily on either side of the Count, Figaro confronted him assured and smiling. It was the smile, perhaps, that unnerved Hans, and caused him to miss the beat on which he should have made his stern attack, flourishing the letter.

First dress rehearsals always go badly, but that was the worst moment of a bad morning. His mind fell blank and his mouth dry; and smiling, helpful, condescending, Marc Chatrier came in for him, prompting him like a Sunday school teacher rescuing a backward boy who has forgotten his catechism:

"'*Cognoscite . . . Signor . . . Figaro . . .*'"

Syllable clearly intoned after syllable, with meaning nods of encouragement, to complete his humiliation. Killing with kindness. The fiery red surged up out of his lace cravat and dyed him crimson to the roots of his hair, but with healthy rage as much as embarrassment. He refused to pick up the proffered thread, looking over his tormentor's shoulder straight into Franz Hassilt's eloquent eyes.

"I am very sorry, that was my fault. Again, please, be so kind!"

This time his blood was up, and he made a good job

of it. No Figaro had ever been bawled out with more authority.

There was no doubt about which side the women were on; they hovered caressingly, complimenting the scowling Count with speaking eyes all the while they were conspiring with his manservant against him. Tonda leaned close to one elbow, Inga hung upon the other arm. And the red in the Count's cheeks did not subside, it merely changed in some subtle way to a milder and more pleasurable shade.

If he only knew, thought Hero critically, hugging her knees in Johnny's stage box, what an ass he looked, shiny with complacency at being courted by two goddesses at once, publicly and blatantly—like a ridiculous latter-day Paris! Uncomfortable he might be, but he couldn't help being flattered even in his discomfort. And she had carefully dissociated herself from the contest, ostentatiously flourished her boyishness under his nose off-stage as well as on, and where had it got her? Had he relaxed with her? He had, and only too thoroughly!

He proceeded to demonstrate it by taking refuge with her in the box as soon as they drew the act to a close and were released for a quarter of an hour's break after their labours. He climbed in to her over the front of the box from the stage, none too deftly because of his elaborate breeches and stiff embroidered coat-skirts. He didn't mind being clumsy in front of her; he would have minded very much if she'd been Tonda or Inga.

He was still flushed, but he'd got over his anger; the twin pussies had purred him into a good humour and an excellent conceit of himself.

"*Himmel!*" he said in a great sigh of relief, and dropped into the seat beside her.

"You made a fine idiot of yourself that time," said Hero, with the unflattering candour that was expected of her.

"I know it! What will Franz say to me when he gets me alone? But now I am all right. It will not happen again."

"Well, they certainly did their best to kiss it better," agreed Hero, straddling the crimson plush rail with the studied maleness she had cultivated for Cherubino's sake until it was almost second nature. "You know, you'll really have to put 'em out of their agony soon. You can't have both, my boy. Take one and let the other go. This is *Figaro*, not *Seraglio*."

And he was fool enough to do it, she thought bitterly, if only he could make up his mind which. Luckily he couldn't. And they were both at least twelve years older than he was!

He turned and gave her a speculative look and a tempted grin. "You want I should drop you overboard, Master Cherubino? With your commission also?"

"You and how many more?" said Hero derisively.

He could move fast enough when he chose, but she could have ducked and rolled out of reach if she had really wished. He held her between large, well-shaped and very capable hands, dangling her backwards over the rim of the box. Oh, yes, she'd succeeded in putting him at his ease with her, all right! She tried to reach his chest with her small fists, but he had her fast by the upper arms, and all she could reach was the satin of his sleeves.

" Let me up, you big ape! I'm falling! "

" Only as far as I shall let you. You are quite safe. Beg my pardon nicely for being impudent! "

But she didn't; and as soon as she allowed the hint of a whimper to complicate her breathless laughter he hoisted her gently back into the box, shifting one hand to a fistful of her hair. He shook her by it softly, and let it go without so much as noticing that it was a fascinating colour between corn and honey, and very thick and fine. No, she'd miscalculated badly, these tactics were getting her nowhere. He never really saw her at all.

However, she probed forward experimentally to be sure of her ground.

" A good thing for you," she said, shaking her ruffles back into order, "that I'm not the predatory type, too."

" Dear God, yes! " he said, with such heartfelt gratitude that she turned open-mouthed to stare at him, suspicious for a moment of such improbable simplicity; but his face was as open as a sunflower at noon, and fervently friendly.

She could hardly believe it. Could anyone really be as modest as that in his disarming vanity?

" At least you feel safe with *me*, don't you? " she said with wincing care. The note that should have warned him crept in, all the same, withering the edges of the words like frost browning the rim of a leaf. But he never noticed it.

" But of course! " he said blithely.

So that was that. He meant it; he had no qualms at all.

That was one plan cancelled; and now something

drastic would have to be done to shake him out of his complacency and make him take another look at what he was slighting. No use turning feminine now, that would only make her one of three in pursuit of him, and lose her even this maddening intimacy which was all she'd gained. No, let him stay feeling safe until he began to feel himself injured and deprived by his security. She could be as feminine as she pleased with someone else; not exactly under his nose, but somewhere just in the corner of his vision.

She cast one comprehensive glance over the available field, and there was only one man in it at all suitable for her purpose. Her grey eyes lingered speculatively on Marc Chatrier's straight shoulders and long, erect back, so elegantly filling the coat of the Count's gentleman's gentleman. Maybe Hans would wake up if she began to demonstrate that a man with twice his experience found her irresistible.

And she wouldn't even have to make the running. As soon as she turned her serious consideration upon Marc Chatrier she became aware what extremely serious consideration he was devoting to her.

" The poor man's Glyndebourne, Johnny calls it," said Hero over coffee. " It was Gisela who started him on opera. She told him I had a good ear and a good voice, and he ought to have me properly taught. And he did, and it turned out opera was what I was best suited for, as well as what I wanted most. So he took up opera and fell wildly in love with it. He built the Leander, and got Franz to take over the musical direction, and we were off. *Hellespont* was the name of his ship, you know, the one he lost the last year of the war." That's why it had to be the Leander Theatre."

"And that's why you are Hero?"

"Oh, yes, that was inevitable. The *Hellespont* changed Johnny's life, it comes out like a rash all over. She was torpedoed, you know, blown to shreds. They lost half the crew, and a lot of the others were disabled. Well, you've seen them. You must have noticed Sam Priddy, the lame one. Chief deck-hand, so to speak. He was Johnny's bos'n, with him all through the war. They think the world of each other."

"So that explains your rather startling staff," said Chatrier, smiling. "I won't pretend I hadn't wondered."

"Yes, well . . . We're nice," said Hero firmly, speaking up loyally for her family, "but let's face it, we *are* a bit odd. There's Sam, and there's Dolly Glazier——her husband was drowned when the *Hellespont* went down. And there's Stoker Bates, who has only one hand, and Chips, and Mateo. And there's Codger Bayliss, the big one who sits in Sam's box and knits. Codger was torpedoed once before he came to Johnny's crew, and then again with the *Hellespont*, and he was about forty hours in the water that time before they found him. They didn't think he'd live, but he did, only now he can't speak, and the shock did something to his mind. We taught him to knit to keep him busy and happy. It's the one new skill he's managed to pick up since it happened to him, and he's so proud of it he almost never stops. Haven't you noticed how many sweaters we all have?"

He laughed. "Your father seems to have had an adventurous war."

"Oh, he did. They were on secret duties, a sort of roving commission. Suited them, they were all born anarchists. They brought out no end of people from occupied Europe, you know. Gisela was one of them," said Hero proudly.

" She was? " A flicker in the dark eyes. " I didn't know that."

" She had some heel of a husband who divorced her as soon as she became a bit of a drag on his career— she's half-Jewish, you see. She'd have gone to Ravensbruck if it hadn't been for Johnny."

" No wonder," said Chatrier softly, " no wonder she's become such a devoted friend to him."

" Gisela's a darling," said Hero warmly. " And she did something just as wonderful for him when she introduced him to opera. She never expected him to go head over heels for it like he did, or to launch out and build an opera house of his own. But Johnny had so much money he didn't know what to do with it. And nothing was too good for me, being the only child, you see."

The kind, attentive, flattering eyes which had been praising her silently all through lunch did not change their expression, yet her thumbs pricked suddenly. Nothing, just a shiver of awareness. A slight, infinitely slight tremor of response to those words of power, "only child" and "money." It illuminated everything, the expert compliments, the indulgent attentions he had been paying her.

She thought, no, I'm imagining it! He's world-famous, he has plenty of money already, why should he care? He just likes me, and enjoys playing with the children, that's all. But the obstinate seed of doubt would not be quieted. Had he necessarily got plenty of money, just because he ranked amongst the greatest

singers of the world? He must have made plenty, but
that was another matter; probably he spent it as fast
as he made it. And when you're—what would he be?
Forty-eight or forty-nine?—when you're nearly fifty
you can't reckon on the funds being inexhaustible for
ever. And then, an opera house thrown in!

Well, she would soon see. If he stopped to speak
kindly to Codger Bayliss, now that she'd clearly
demonstrated her own partiality, she would know
exactly why.

And he did. Somehow she had been sure he would.

Codger was alone in Sam's room by the stage-door,
knitting away for dear life, and he lifted his fine, blank
eyes at them as they came by, and focused upon Hero
the sudden, struggling glimmer of recognition and love
that belonged to all Johnny's chattels. The hands that
shook and dangled aimlessly when they were dis-
engaged, with an almost spastic compulsion, were
steady enough on the steel needles. He was clean and
closely shaved, and always neat in his person; Sam saw
to that, and the legacy of the navy years helped. The
big, well-shaped head with its motionless features might
have been carved in wood, except when convulsed with
the effort at speech, eternally painful and vain.

" That's a splendid pattern," said Chatrier gently,
halting to smile at him and finger the green pullover.
" Some day, if I earn the favour, I'm going to ask you
to knit one like it for me."

Very nicely done, the touch and the voice. Like those
odious people who take children on their knees to
ingratiate themselves with their mothers, though they
don't want them, and the children don't want to be
nursed. Such people ought always to be confronted,

and indeed usually are, with just such a cold, distant
stare.

So now she knew. It came as a shock to her vanity
to realise that the man she had been making use of was
also making use of her. But at least it eased her conscience of the slight compunction she had felt towards
him.

They went on along the corridor to the stairs. Twice
he allowed his hand to touch hers, and each time closed
his fingers momentarily and very delicately, as though
the touch had been accidental, and his elaboration of it
a motion of deference and apology.

" Hero———"

He drew her to a halt in the dimmest corner, and she
turned to face him, speculating behind a placid face on
what might be coming next. It was too soon yet for
extremes, unless he thought her very impressionable.

" Hero, if you're free this evening will you come and
have dinner with me in town? I should like just once
to be quiet with you, before the excitement begins.
Drive in with me after rehearsal. I'll bring you back
in good time."

" Oh, no, I should have to go home and change," she
objected, fending off the necessity for answering with a
definite yes or no. " I couldn't possibly show up at the
Grand Eden without my best frock. And I did half-
promise to look in on my grandmother to-night."

" Come later, then, come for dinner at any rate.
Grandmothers should be in bed early. She'll spare you
by eight o'clock? "

She clutched at that. By eight o'clock she would
surely have made up her mind, and if she wanted to
back out she could think of some excuse, telephone him.

All she wanted now was not to have to promise to go
with him, to have time to think. "Yes, I could
probably make it by eight. Yes, I'm sure I could."

"Good, then I shall expect you at eight. You won't
forget?"

Probably she would have let it rest at that, if her
quick ear had not caught and understood the faint creak
of the stage-door swinging as someone with a light, long
step bounded in from the street.

She knew that gait very well. Suddenly she lifted her
face with the defenceless confiding of a child, in a half-
invitation there was no mistaking. She saw Chatrier's
eyes kindle warmly in self-congratulation, and momentarily closed her own, as he drew her gently to him by
the shoulders, and kissed her on the mouth.

Only when the hasty footsteps rounded the corner
and baulked wildly, did Chatrier disengage himself and
turn, too late to see more than a hastily receding back
in a light raincoat.

Hero, emerging from the kiss chilled and stiff with
doubt and self-reproach, caught one fleeting glimpse
of Hans Selverer's face as he skidded to a halt, hung for
one instant dumbfounded and motionless, and then
spread a hand against the wall, swung round, and
retreated precipitately round the corner. If it was any
satisfaction to her, at least he'd seen her this time. She
carried the vision of his outraged and startled face with
her as she drew herself quickly away and turned to
scurry up the stairs.

"You won't forget?" said Chatrier, letting her go
by stages, his fingers slipping smoothly down her arm.

"I won't forget," she said, and ran for her dressing-
room.

It was what she'd wanted, what she'd intended to happen; yet now she wished it undone. It wasn't the thought of Hans that had shaken her with this sudden storm of doubt and dismay, it was the memory of the embrace she had just provoked, so accomplished, so restrained, so gentle, so calculated. It was the first time in her life she had ever been kissed without the least trace of affection, and it had made her aware that she was playing with something considerably more dangerous than fire.

All the same, she wasn't giving up now, whatever the hazards. Not when Hans Selverer was just beginning to notice her existence!

" Pay Johnny to keep an eye on that little madam," said Sam Priddy, watching them pass singly across the end of the corridor and climb the stairs; first the girl, flushed and in a hurry, then the man, at leisure and smiling faintly, the light of amusement and satisfaction in his eyes.

" She's all right," said Stoker Bates comfortably. " Our kid's got all her buttons on, don't you worry."

" I know she has. But that's one bloke I don't like, that Chatrier. Johnny should have left him where he was, as good a Figaro as he may be. Asks too many questions round here, and answers too few."

" He can sing like nobody's business," said Stoker positively.

" He can that, I don't deny it. But he treats young Hans like a half-witted beginner, and he's pretty off-hand with Miss Salberg, too. And now he's making a dead set at Butch. I don't like it. And the hell of it is," said Sam, tugging irritably at his thick grey hair,

" I keep thinking I've seen that superior pan of his somewhere afore. What's more, I believe Johnny has the same idea. I've seen him looking sideways at the bloke sometimes, as though he was bashing his brains to remember where he'd run up against him, and couldn't fix it. Maybe it's only an illusion, maybe we're just recalling photographs we've seen of him, or something. I just wish I could feel sure about it, that's all. I just wish I knew."

CHAPTER TWO

" I SHALL BE OUT to-night, darling," said Hero, half-obscured by the cloud of fair hair she was industriously brushing. The powdered wig was hot to wear, and crushed her feather cut. She kicked off Cherubino's buckled shoes, and sank on to the stool before her mirror. " I've got a dinner date, but I promise I won't be late back."

Johnny, half-submerged in the big tub chair by the window, looked up sharply.

" Who're you meeting?"

It didn't occur to him, until she turned to stare, how far he was stepping out of character. He never asked her where she had been, or with whom, he'd never had to. Usually she told him, and if she didn't it was because she forgot, and then he trusted her. And now suddenly he sat upright and bristled at the mention of an unnamed date, and wondered that she gaped at him almost anxiously, as though he'd shown signs of growing old, or sickening for something.

" I like to know these things, Butch," he said placatingly, subsiding again, but warily. " Fathers get that way. You wouldn't be flattered if I just said: O.K., push off, who cares!"

" Johnny, dear," said Hero, levelling her hairbrush at him admonishingly, " I'm getting a big girl now."

" I know," said Johnny moodily, " that's the trouble. Other people are beginning to notice it. And since we're

34

on this subject, let's say it right out loud—you're a well-heeled girl, too."

She finished arranging her hair, and said nothing. He waited, growing a little anxious but sure he wouldn't have to insist; but when she still said nothing he pursued doggedly: "So who're you meeting?"

She didn't know why she hadn't told him at once; there must be something very slightly wrong with her conscience. Surely there was no reason in the world why he should be displeased, and yet she knew he would be. And she'd begun this all wrong in any case, because she hadn't even made up her mind whether to go or not.

She eyed her father in the mirror, steadily and warningly, and said: "It's Mr. Chatrier, if you want to know."

Johnny came out the chair as if he'd been stung, and hung over his daughter stiff with dismay, but not, she noted, with surprise. This was what he'd had in mind when he popped up like a jack-in-the-box and scowled at her.

"Oh, it is, is it?" said Johnny ominously. "Well, let me tell you something, Hero Truscott. I've been hearing things already about your goings-on with the great Figaro, and that's one association I'd rather see kept strictly professional. You hear?"

All she had really heard was the offensive description of her strategy, and she took fire at it. If there had been no goings-on at all—as indeed there so nearly had— she would have laughed at him and probably reassured him; but the one kiss, so clearly invited, stuck fast in her mind and wouldn't be swallowed down. She turned on him with all the rage of her sore conscience.

" Goings-on! Johnny Truscott, them's fighting words! So you've been hearing things, have you? You never had the decency to come to me and say so straight out, and ask me what I had to say, did you? What am I supposed to have done? Go on, tell me! And who runs with the tales? Somebody with a pretty vivid imagination—and you swallow every word, I suppose."

It had only just dawned on her that one person at least might have something factual to report, and her eyes and mouth rounded with indignation. " Well, the stodgy great prig! " she gasped. " Just wait till I see him! "

" You leave Sam alone, he never said a word against you, *I*'m the one who called them *your* goings-on. Sam was only worried about you getting hurt. And why shouldn't he be? And why shouldn't he talk to me about it? "

" Oh," said Hero in a subsiding breath, and smiled again for a fleeting minute, " oh, *Sam*! "

" What do you mean—' *Oh, Sam*? ' Dolly as well, if you must know. Damn it, we all take an interest in what you do, how can we help it? Anyhow, I've been noticing things myself the last couple of days. And I don't want you to spend your time with Chatrier. He's old enough to be your father, and let him sing as well as he will, he's a man I find I don't like. You be friendly with him while you're at work, but don't get involved with him." He linked his hands under her chin and turned up her face to him, smiling down at her anxiously, willing to be conciliatory if only she'd help him. " You won't go, will you, Butch? Ring him up later, and say you've got a headache."

" Johnny! What a dirty trick! "

She had to sound scandalised, because it was exactly what she'd been thinking of doing; and no sooner had she given utterance to this judgment than she had to accept it. She would go. Why shouldn't she? If she didn't she would be wasting all the trouble she'd already taken, and Hans would soon forget the salutary shock of seeing her devoting to someone else attentions she never bothered to lavish on him.

" I promised to go," she said, all the more firmly because it was not strictly true.

" Well, you can easily get out of it——"

" And I *want* to go."

" Then this time," said Johnny flatly, " want will be your master, that's all."

" Are you telling me I can't go? " She couldn't believe it, such a thing had never arisen between them before, and she didn't know how to deal with it without being furiously angry or melting into tears from pure shock.

" Just that! I'm forbidding you to go."

He didn't trust her! After all the years he'd known her, he couldn't rely on her to have a sense of values, to know what Marc Chatrier was and rate him accordingly. That was what hurt her most, that and the sting of knowing that she was to blame, and he was at any rate partially justified. Worse, he was justified without knowing it. And now she was fairly in it, and she had to go, or lose her self-respect for ever. Johnny's daughter couldn't back out, and mustn't admit defeat.

" I'm going! " she said.

" Is that so? " said Johnny, his own temper flaring. " Now, look, I'm giving you one minute to see sense and promise me you'll ring him and call it off."

" Why should I ? I'm nineteen, and I've never given you reason . . . You've no *right* to be like this. All I'm going to do is have dinner with him, what is there in that ? If you think you're going to begin choosing my friends for me at *this* stage, Johnny Truscott, you can damn' well think again."

" You're going nowhere but home to-night," said Johnny, sticking out his jaw. " Make up your mind to that."

" Oh, yes, I am, I'm going to the Grand Eden. Try and stop me ! "

" I mean to," he said promptly, and turned and plunged upon her clothes, that lay in a frothy little pile upon a chair. He scooped them up in one arm, wrenched open the wardrobe and gathered her dress and coat from their hangers. She flew to intercept him, but he evaded her with a swerve that would have done credit to a rugby forward, and was out of the room with her stockings floating behind him.

The door slammed; incredulously she heard the key turn.

She banged furiously on the panels for one moment, and then gave up. This time he'd gone too far. He expected her to laugh, and rage, and argue, and finally allow herself to be appeased and cajoled into giving way gracefully. He'd find out his mistake. She wasn't his daughter for nothing.

She stood silent, glaring at the door, beyond which the expectant silence gradually lengthened out into an uneasy hush. She could practically see him standing there, the pig-headed old autocrat, waiting for her to speak first.

At last he drummed his fingertips suggestively

against the door, and said in a carefully level voice that couldn't quite disguise his baffled disquiet: " I'll be back in an hour. If you're ready to talk sense then you can come out."

Poor Johnny, he'd wanted the whole thing to break down in laughter, maybe even in a rough-and-tumble, so that they could go off home cronies as thick as ever. She steeled her heart and said equally constrainedly: " And if I'm not? "

" Then you can stay there till you are."

" You'd better start phoning round for a substitute Cherubino, then," said Hero coldly. " Good night! Don't bother to come back in an hour, you'll only be wasting your time."

Johnny exploded with the kind of oath he thought he'd forgotten, and stamped away along the corridor and left her to her obstinacy. The toe of a nylon drooped derisively from the crack of the door. She damned it and sat down to scowl at her own face in the mirror. Now how on earth had all that come about, when neither of them had wanted it?

She curled up in the tub chair and waited for Johnny to come back, sure of his surrender if only she stood her ground.

He made her wait the full hour, and then she heard his fingers rap softly at the door again. Cajolingly, close to the panel, he said: " Butch! "

No answer.

" You ready to come home yet? " coaxed Johnny.

" On what terms? " said Hero.

" Now don't be an ass. What's so important about this business, anyhow? "

" The principle," said Hero grimly.

" All right, then! On *my* terms. You stop this
nonsense and come home with me, or I'll leave you here
until after the performance to-night, and see how you
like that," said Johnny, beginning to shout again, " you
obstinate little hellion! "

" Good night," said Hero; and Johnny went.

Now she'd really done it. He wouldn't come back
until the house lights went out for the night, and then,
in a way, he'd have won, and that was unthinkable. She
couldn't get out, no use even shouting for someone else,
because Johnny'd taken the key. She'd be late for her
date now in any case. And she had no clothes, and if
she sneaked back to the house to change she might get
caught. Even supposing she could get out in the first
place, which she couldn't.

It took her half an hour more to remember the
hatches Johnny had had run through the walls in the
three end dressing-rooms on this side, because the
windows were not suitable for an outside fire escape.
They had never been used, and no one thought of them;
even Johnny had forgotten. But there in the corner was
the low square trap, and all she had to do was slip
through it into the dressing-room next door and walk
out blithely into the corridor.

It was as simple as that! And as for clothes—well,
these were good enough for the eighteenth century, why
not for the twentieth?

Her eyes had begun to dance as soon as she saw her
way to a victory. She scrambled back into Cherubino's
embroidered coat, smoothed on the powdered wig with
its neat black ribbon queue, and shot her ruffles with a
swagger in the mirror. Gleaming pale-blue satin
breeches, white silk stockings, black buckled shoes, full

shirt-sleeves knotted with black ribbon billowing in the
wide cuffs of the sky-blue coat, and pearl-grey waistcoat
stiff with silver thread. Nothing could possibly be more
respectable.

No, wait a minute, why not go the whole hog? Off
came the coat again, and she settled the ribbon of rainbow silk that was the baldric of Cherubino's smallsword
across the breast of the silver waistcoat, and eased the
scabbard comfortably at her hip. The finishing touch.

This she was really looking forward to. This would
be the biggest free publicity stunt any première of
Figaro had ever had, and Johnny could like it or lump
it, whichever he liked.

She twisted the full skirts of her coat before the
mirror a last time, clapped the silver-braided tricorne
on top of her wig, and slid open the panel in the wall.

" West End, here I come! " said Hero, and ducked
through the hatch and ran for the back staircase.

The commissionaire who opened the door of the
Aston Martin in front of the discreetly lit portal of the
hotel gaped and stared for an instant at the vision that
slid nimbly out of the car. Two leather-coated young
men halted and whistled, and even respectable elderly
gentlemen turned their heads and loitered to watch,
faint grins of pleasure and speculation dawning gently
on their disillusioned faces. London, accustomed to
every fantastic manner of dress the world provides,
sometimes still shows mild surprise and sophisticated
wonder at the tricks chance can play.

Most of those who lingered to admire Hero's vain-
glorious progress up the steps and in at the glass doors
put her down to the vagaries of the film world or the

advertising business, but that did not lessen the pleasure
she gave them.

The diminutive page-boy who was just crossing the
foyer as she entered had more imagination. At first
sight of her his jaw dropped so far that he almost dislodged his pill-box cap, but the next moment he had
laid a white-gloved paw on his heart and swept her a
prodigious bow.

" Good evening, m'lord! "

Hero twirled her ruffles and flourished her hat, and
made him an even more elaborate return, and they
parted with solemn faces, magnificent in make-believe.
After that the grown-ups with their goggling astonishment, smoothly hooded at once behind professional
serenity, were a sad come-down. The middle-aged
gentlemen sitting over drinks in the open hall showed
candid appreciation, but she ignored them; in or out
of fancy dress, they were easy game.

The women were more interesting. Eyebrows
signalled indulgent amusement, mild curiosity, and
cool, well-bred, expertly disguised jealousy. Hero
slowed her progress towards the reception desk to give
them their money's worth, and accentuated the delicate
swagger she had cultivated for Cherubino until she had
every eye in the room upon her. It was good practice
for achieving the same effect on the stage. It was also
slightly alarming, and very pleasant.

Two round, dark waiters, plainly Italian, achieved
the feat of pouring out drinks flawlessly while their eyes
followed her with eloquent and perfectly frank delight
the length of the room. A male clerk had mysteriously
materialised from some hidden regions, and unobtru-
sively elbowed the woman aside from the precise area

of the desk at which the vision might be expected to arrive. An invisible spotlight accompanied her. All the other women might as well not have been there at all, nobody was looking at them.

She was very late, presumably Chatrier had given her up. She leaned a satin elbow on the desk, tilted her smallsword cockily, and said nonchalantly: " Will you be so kind as to acquaint Mr. Chatrier with my arrival? He expected me earlier, but unfortunately I was unavoidably delayed."

" Certainly, *sir*! " said the goggle-eyed clerk, a shade heavy-handed with his co-operation. " What name shall I say? "

" Cherubino," she said grandly, and turned to let her gaze rove tranquilly over the audience in the foyer.

She had practically put a stop to conversation there, even business held its breath a little. One of the Italian waiters moved slowly out of sight through a service door, his chin on his shoulder, and his eyes devouring her to the last moment when the door swung to between them.

A tall young man had just come in from the dining-room, and was looking round in some wonder for the focus of the prevalent hush. He found it, and halted as abruptly as if he had run his good-looking nose into a brick wall. The blue eyes opened very wide, directing at her a long, roused, dubious stare. Better and better! She had forgotten in her single-minded obstinacy that most of the company's principals, including Hans Selverer, were at the same hotel.

She continued to gaze past him, contemplating the florid decoration of the far wall, but acutely aware of what was going on behind his cloudy face, none the

less. He was making up his mind; he was beginning
to thread his way between the chairs and tables towards
her. Not yet, she thought firmly, and not here, and
turned again to the beaming clerk, who was just
cradling the telephone.

" Mr. Chatrier will come down at once."

He was coming down at that very moment, and
precipitately.

The first glimpse of his face was interesting. Through
the blaze of conscientious delight she sensed the careful
motions of a mind busy balancing solid satisfaction at
her coming, with all its implications, against irritation
at the difficulty in which she'd landed him. This was
far too public and unorthodox for his plans. She'd alert
her father too soon—if, indeed, she hadn't done so
already.

" Hero, my dear! " He took her hands, looking her
over with magnificently dissembled dismay. " I'd given
you up. What has happened? "

" I know," she said quickly. " I'm sorry, I couldn't
get away earlier." Out of the tail of her eye she
observed that Chatrier's arrival had stopped Hans
Selverer in his tracks. He frowned, hesitating whether
to meddle; if she wasn't quick he'd make up his
deliberate but formidable mind and move in on the spot,
and Johnny might take a dim view of his daughter
playing the leading part in a public scene.

" Can we go somewhere quiet? " she said appeal-
ingly. " I didn't really *want* to sail in here looking like
a refugee from pantomime."

" Of course! Come up to my suite, I'll have them
bring dinner there for you."

He shepherded her hastily up the staircase in his arm,

bending over her with elderly gallantry for the benefit
of the spectators. The gallantry he would display upstairs would probably be of another kind, though
equally discreet and expert, but with Hans Selverer's
black scowl scorching her back she felt pretty secure.
The only question was whether, between the two of
them, she would get any dinner that night, and that
represented a risk she felt to be justified in the circumstances.

" I'm afraid," said Chatrier softly in her ear, " you've
been running into rough water for my sake. Come and
tell me. If there's something wrong I must know. I
don't want to complicate your life."

Somewhere in the velvet solicitude of his voice there
was hidden a thin, clear stream of silent thought that
she could almost translate aloud. This girl is going to
be a push-over. She wouldn't have come here like this,
nuisance though she is, if she hadn't got it badly. Take
it easy to-night, but better get her tied up quickly and
irrevocably, so that marriage on civilised terms will
seem the best thing even to her father.

The sudden chill of warning trickled down her spine.
If she had been less sure of Hans Selverer, gnawing his
lip down there in the foyer, she would have turned back
then.

She needn't have worried. The tap at the door of the
sitting-room came before they had even finished the
first drink. She had had, as it happened, no intention
of finishing hers; she knew her limitations, and she
knew a calculated inhibition-loosener when she tasted
one. Chatrier had seemed, if anything, rather relieved
to see her lack of interest in it. Probably the drinks had

been ordered beforehand, and he had regretted his too-comprehensive planning when he guessed that Johnny was already in arms. Possibly he was as relieved as she was when the door, opening in response to his invitation, admitted Hans Selverer instead of the expected waiter.

" Please forgive this intrusion," said Hans, closing the door firmly behind him, " but I have a message for Miss Truscott from her father." He fixed his eyes upon Hero, curled in the deep chair with the half-emptied glass at her elbow, and set his young jaw at her like a bulldog. " I have told him that you are here, and quite safe. I think you must know that he has been looking for you everywhere, and was very alarmed about you. I have reassured him that you are about to leave for home. Under my escort."

" You have," said Marc Chatrier, coming hotly to his feet, " the impudence of the devil, Mr. Selverer."

But he hesitated then, visibly checking his natural anger in face of a sudden doubt. He turned upon Hero, too; he came across to her and stood looking down at her with a slight, troubled frown.

" Hero, you didn't tell me that your father had no idea you were here. Is it true? "

The part was developing real possibilities. She hugged her satin knees and lowered her eyes uneasily, admiring Chatrier's resourcefulness and her own versatility. She hedged, protesting that she had been about to tell him the whole story, that Johnny must have *known* where she would be, though actually—well, there'd been no time, she'd just hopped into the car and come. Why not? What difference did it make?

The cue was admirably taken.

" What *difference!* " sighed Chatrier. " Oh, my dear girl! You should have told me. How can I possibly . . ."

He turned away with a small gesture of gentle exasperation, and came eye to eye with Hans, who had not moved from his place by the door.

" You say you've spoken to Mr. Truscott? Why did you not have the courtesy to speak first to me? You must have known that I would not dream of doing anything behind his back. What have you told him? "

" Simply that Miss Truscott is here. I dissuaded him," said Hans grimly, " from leaping into his car and coming to fetch her, but he made it plain that he did not know she was here, and did not wish her to remain. He has authorised me to drive her home, and I shall do so."

" I'm not coming! " said Hero loudly and indignantly.

She didn't really want a fight, she wasn't sure that she could cope with it, though the potentialities had a certain allure; but it would look altogether too complacent in her if she fell into line without putting up a struggle.

" Yes," said Hans, very pale and very precise, " you will come."

" I won't! And please go away. Your interference in my affairs is insufferable."

" I am sorry. All the same, you are going home." He grew grimmer by the moment. " After that you need not be troubled with me any more."

She was comfortably certain that he didn't mean it; his voice held too much vehemence and too little conviction. She began to look forward ardently to that drive home, and didn't know for the life of her how to get to it gracefully; but she need not have worried, Chatrier was equal to this as to all situations.

" Hero," he said very gently and reasonably, leaning down to take her by the shoulders, " you don't realise. This is something I can't countenance. I had no intention of deceiving your father, and we must put it right at once. This young man may be insufferable, as you say, but he is undoubtedly right. You must go home. I would take you myself, but your father wishes and expects that you should go with Selverer, and I have no right whatever to quarrel with what your father wants."

He drew her to her feet, kindly but firmly, smiled at her, and turned to cast one light, disparaging glance over the stiff young sentry by the door. " You will undoubtedly be quite safe with Selverer," he said.

Who would have thought that could be turned into such a deadly insult? And one that couldn't be resented, either. Hans reddened slowly to his hair, but said not a word.

" So, please, dear child," said Chatrier, turning his back scornfully on his enemy, " do as I ask you, and as you know you ought to. Go home and make your peace with your father. You will be glad afterwards."

She let herself be persuaded. " Well—if *you* say so." Disconsolate, devoted, all he could wish. A push-over.

He escorted her to the door, and there, as though there had been no uncompromising figure grimly guarding it, he kissed her lightly on the forehead. Oh, the fatherliness of it, the forebearance, the breathtaking hypocrisy! " Good night, Hero! "

" Good night! " she said, gruff and small, and went out meekly with Hans watchful at her elbow.

On the stairs he took her by the arm, and she felt what did not show in his face, the full tension of his rage. He was furiously angry with her, she had only to prod him a little and the fire would blaze. This was better than that young-brother stuff at least, this was something she could enjoy; and now that she was out of Chatrier's sight she needn't even contain her enjoyment.

She hardly felt the reviving glances that provided a guard of honour for her exit, and Hans was not aware of them at all. The first check came when he had marched her out at the door and down the steps to the Aston Martin. He transferred to her the glower he had fixed on the car.

" Your key, please! "

She gave it to him, trying not to look too complacent about it. " Like me to drive? " she said innocently.

For answer he opened the passenger door for her, and bundled her into the seat, slamming the door upon her with the first tremor of temper he had betrayed. He settled himself beside her dourly, and switched on the engine.

" Are you sure you can drive it? "

He approached it with caution, but he soon showed her if he could drive it. Once he had got the feel of it, she had never been whisked out of London at a smarter pace. True, he set off at first in the wrong direction, his experience of the streets of London being sketchy as yet; and when she thought fit to point it out, he extricated himself from a one-way street by means of a U-turn which would have landed him in court if there had been a policeman handy; but of his technical ability there could be no doubt.

" You're still going the wrong way," said Hero helpfully.

" You will please direct me," he said through his teeth.

" Why should I? " she objected reasonably. " I'm in no hurry to get home. You're the one who said we were going there. I don't mind if we end up in Bath—and we shall, if you keep tearing along the A4 at this rate."

Hans braked suddenly and brought the car to the side of the road. He turned on her furiously; even in the dark she felt the blue, outraged glare he fixed on her.

" Everything is play to you. You are *irresponsible*. To come here to London *so*, when you knew your father did not wish it, and to allow yourself to go to that man's room like—like———"

" Be careful! " said Hero, flaring dangerously.

"—like a half-witted *child*. And all out of vanity, because you must have your own way. You don't care that your father is worried and waits for you. You don't care what trouble you cause, only *you* must be amused and indulged. And so *stupid*, to put yourself in the hands of such a man."

" What's the matter with him? What have you got against him? So far he's behaved towards me a great deal more considerately than you ever have, you—you virtuous busybody! That's what you are, a meddlesome, priggish busybody! "

" And you," he said furiously, " are a spoiled, self-willed, ill-natured *child*! Your father should *beat* you."

" Why don't you advise him to? You fancy yourself at correcting other people's behaviour, why stop at

mine? You could put him wise to his parental mistakes
—maybe he'd be more grateful than I am."

For a moment she thought he was going to take her
by the shoulders and shake her, at the very least;
instead, he jerked away from her with a set face, and
seized the wheel.

"I must go more to the left. You will tell me where
to turn, or else I will lock you in the car while I go to
telephone your father and tell him where we are."

That wouldn't have suited her, but not for the reason
he supposed. She had still several miles of wrangling
to look forward to, as things were, and she hadn't half-
finished the fight yet. So she told him, only prolonging
the ride by a few modest prevarications here and there.
The battle raged every yard of the way, and was the
most gratifying event of her day. Whatever he felt
towards her now, it wasn't indifference; and it wasn't
the blind, benevolent affection of an elder brother,
either.

The battle with Johnny was less satisfactory. For one
thing, he had been really frightened, when he weakened
and went back to release her, only to find her gone; and
that made her feel horribly guilty. For another, he was
still blinder than any bat, and that infuriated her so
much that she had no difficulty in transferring the load
of her guilt to him.

He ought to have known her better, after all they'd
been to each other all her life. He ought to have been
looking for her real motives—no, he ought to have felt
them by instinct, without even having to look for them.
He ought to have recognised that admittedly hare-
brained trip to London as what it was, a commando raid

into enemy territory, undertaken for strategic reasons—
well, partly strategic and partly prestige. After all, he
had practically dared her to do it. And here he was,
fussing and lecturing in a heavy-handed way, actually
convinced that she was genuinely infatuated with Marc
Chatrier.

It hadn't occurred to her until then that anyone but
Marc Chatrier himself, and with luck Hans Selverer,
could seriously believe that she was attracted to the man.
And that Johnny should swallow it so easily, Johnny of
all people! She felt as if a gulf had suddenly yawned
between them, the revelation set him so far from her.

She had walked straight into his arms on arrival, and
kissed him, and apologised for scaring him, all in the
best filial style, more than willing to make amends, but
desiring also that he should admit his own folly. And
now where were they?

She'd never thought the day would come when she'd
heard Johnny carrying on like a father. And no end to
it! She finished the sandwiches she'd brought in with
her providently from the kitchen, and poured the last
cup of coffee.

"You ought to take lessons from Hans," she said
bitterly. "You ask him, some time, how to deal with
daughters. He knows it all."

"Now, Butch," said Johnny reproachfully, "do I
deserve that tone? I can't help being anxious, when I
see you going overboard for a man I don't like and don't
trust. You take my word for it, he isn't worth any hard
words between you and me——"

"God!" said Hero incredulously. "We sound like
a cut-price soap opera."

"You're only just nineteen," said Johnny doggedly,

" and I'm responsible for you, and whether you find it corny or not, my girl, I'm going to *be* responsible for you. You think about it overnight, and don't kid yourself I'm fooling. If you're not to be trusted with a car, right, I'll get rid of the Aston, and if you're not to be trusted with money to spend I'll tie up your allowance so you can't get at it."

That did it. Outraged, Hero marched across the hearth to stare him closely and fiercely in the eye. It wasn't the threat that infuriated her, it was his sheer, monumental stupidity.

" You can do all that," she said, " but *still* you won't be able to dictate to me whom I shall love—or even like."

" Maybe not," said Johnny, equally grim, " but I can put a whole lot of obstacles in the way of your making a go of it."

" You might alter my ideas about some of the people I *used* to like though," said Hero as a vicious afterthought, and stalked out of the room shaken to the heart by the cruelty of the barb she hadn't even suspected she was going to throw.

Franz Hassilt had called an extra rehearsal for the next morning, bent on worrying out a few rough edges he had detected in the immensely complex and delicate structure of the last act. It went well and ended early; and Marc Chatrier was just opening his late mail in his dressing-room when Johnny Truscott tapped at the door and walked in upon him.

" Can you spare me five minutes? This won't take longer."

He had closed the door behind him with the finality of a man going into action, and his lively, inquisitive face had about it the settled look it must always have worn when he entered dangerous waters. Johnny was as capable of subtlety as anyone, but what he hated was inaction when action was ultimately inevitable. Moving in, he always looked the happier for it.

" At the risk of appearing both obvious and crude," he said, declining the chair Chatrier swung round for him from the table, " I've got something to say to you. Keep away from my daughter."

" At the risk of appearing equally obvious," said Chatrier, suddenly erect and attentive, " I would point out that you seem to have committed your daughter to pretty close contact with me, since you allow her to sing major rôles in your theatre."

" Figaro," said Johnny crisply, " I don't mind. Figaro I can stomach. Chatrier, to be blunt, I can't. And I'm telling you again, leave my girl alone. I pay you what your agent asked, you give me, amply, what I'm paying for. Leave it at that, and we can respect each other and work together. But lay off Hero, or I pitch you out of here, and you can make it cost me what you like, it'll still be very well worth it. And, if you'll overlook a further crudity, the publicity will do you more harm than it will me—the stage you've reached."

" Ah! " said Chatrier in a soft voice, and faintly smiling his ambiguous smile. " It's like that, is it? "

He folded the letter he had been reading, and slipped it back into its envelope with deliberately graceful movements of long, elegantly-shaped fingers.

" My dear Truscott, I am comfortable here, I have no intention of moving out, and none of suing. And I like your daughter."

" That I can believe. But it doesn't alter the way I feel."

"Ah, but isn't the way *she* feels of more importance?"

" Not," said Johnny, " if you want the gold mine as well as the girl. And don't pretend you'd be very interested without it, however much you might like her."

" Oh, come, how little faith you show in the charms of a very delightful young lady."

" I've warned you," said Johnny, unmoved. " I don't say things twice."

He turned and walked to the door, and his hand was already outstretched to open it when the soft voice behind him said conversationally: " How's the export-import business doing, Truscott? How much per body these days, and in and out of where? Or have you become a hundred per cent legitimate? I dare say you're rich enough to be able to afford to."

The door remained closed. Johnny stood a moment with ears pricked, considering the implications, and they spread widening circles into recesses of his life of which he had not thought for a long time.

He turned slowly, and came back into the room, gazing down at Chatrier with a thoughtful face. The agreeable mask, turned up to him smiling, could have been covering a mine of knowledge or a monumental bluff.

" Really well-informed bastards," said Johnny in a sweet, small voice, " talk less."

" They talk just enough to convey what they mean. I can be an interesting conversationalist when I lay myself out to please. Your authorities, for instance, would be interested in some of the stories I could tell about your old passenger lists. There would be names on them they never knew—wouldn't there? Not all those pathetic refugees of yours came in like Gisela, all open and above-board—did they? There were others . . ."

Johnny relaxed his cramped fingers in his trouser-pockets, and wrote off the hope that this was simple bluff. The fellow knew about Gisela. She was all right, she had nothing to hide; nothing about her had ever been hidden, except the worst of her experiences, which she kept for ever to herself. But there had been others. There had indeed!

He remembered a Spaniard, tainted with a mild trade-union background, who had been just one jump ahead of a long prison term, without means, and without a hope of getting legal admittance to Britain. He'd be old now, but he could still be extradited if they caught up with him. And the Algerian girl who was still wanted by the French, if only they had known where to look for her.

Even some of the wartime waifs, whose political past, honest enough and innocent enough in Johnny's eyes, had contained elements which made their admittance by ordinary channels dubious, at a period when there was no time to brief counsel and argue the matter out. And since then, certain scholars and artists of intractably independent mind who would not, simply would not, endorse theories and acts they held to be immoral. A long procession of his crimes passed before his eyes and warmed his heart.

Maybe there were one or two questionable cases among them, but on the whole he was proud of them. Those who could pay had paid, and those who couldn't, hadn't. The costs had been met, somehow. And then, the Palestine days. The active nights along that inhospitable coast, the crowded, passionate, desperate, resolute and tragic cargoes, shaken loose from their past, and bent with all the hoarded fire of their natures upon reaching their future. Of them, too, he thought with pleasure and warmth, and gratitude, too, because they at least were safe, nobody was going to extradite them any more. All they could do, if the record came to light, was sink him in the hottest water of his life. But the others could be hounded out of their new and fragile security back to countries that had ill-used them and codes that were waiting to kill them.

Not, thought Johnny behind his placid face, if I know it.

" You tell me," he said. " It's your story."

Chatrier leaned back in his chair at ease, and lit a cigarette. He was smiling, and the sparkle in his black eyes looked entirely confident, but he was an actor off the stage as well as on, and who could be sure what sort of a hand he really held?

" It would take too long," he said, " and you'd find it tedious. Perhaps just one little instance will settle your mind. You took off a certain party once from Italy, when Mussolini was cracking and the Germans were taking over. I could name the police official in Rome who was your contact and acted as go-between, but names are indiscreet. A fat fellow with a short beard—you remember? "

Johnny continued to regard him with the bright, impartial interest of a helpful pupil taking pity on a dim teacher.

" Yes, I think you remember. They shot him after-

wards, did you know that? There were five people, all
of them artists of one kind or another, all wanted by the
Germans. But they weren't official business, and they
weren't the kind that are easy to dispose of. A travelled
lot, not wanted in several countries. Some of them got
through eventually with legal papers, and some had to
do without. But they all found asylum. Two of them
in this country—and I could name both of them. I
know what else you took aboard, too. Three very
valuable canvases stolen from a German who had himself undoubtedly stolen them in the first place, and
quite an assortment of smaller works of art—most of
them in America now, I should imagine. They'd be
very interested in that privateering sideline, too, but to
do you justice I don't suppose that worries you very
much. But the people, Truscott, the people would
worry you a great deal."

He shouldn't have lingered with such particular
emphasis on his single instance; Johnny had him now.
Eighteen years is a long time, and men change, but it
was not for nothing Johnny had been scouring his
remoter memories for that precise turn of the black
head, and the rich music of the voice.

He hadn't been known as Marc Chatrier then, and
he hadn't yet consolidated even the ground of his
present reputation. Five people, all artists of one kind
or another, and all in imminent danger of arrest; and
one of them a young singer, born in Alsace, admittedly
no hero, admittedly somewhat compromised in his
complaisant dealings with Nazi authority, but due to be
picked up within a day or two, and certain to be done
to death rapidly or slowly thereafter. Johnny groped
after the name, but it still eluded him. The face,

hardened, polished and aged, smiled up at him through the smoke of Chatrier's cigarette from narrowed black eyes.

That made things clearer, if not easier. It meant that he really had knowledge he could use to harm at least two people besides Johnny. But in all probability it also meant that that was the sum of his knowledge.

Did that make him less dangerous? Hardly. What mattered was not what he himself could uncover, but what was there to be uncovered once he set the process in motion. If they followed up one case and found it proved, they would set about stripping all the rest. And even if they stopped at one or two, what use was that? They were none of them expendable.

Johnny relaxed; he knew now where he stood. No need to dispute what they both remembered very well; there were no witnesses.

" Well, well! " he said. " So that's what became of the starved tom-cat baritone from the Rome opera. You *have* got on in the world, haven't you? No wonder I couldn't quite place you. All this time I've been fretting over little things about you, trying to decide who it was you reminded me of. And I shouldn't wonder if you weren't on the run at all, if only I'd had time to go into it a bit more thoroughly."

" Oh, yes, I was on the run, and only just ahead of the axe, too. It was a little private matter that had made Rome too hot to hold me—a little affair of a woman who belonged to a German general."

" It would be! " said Johnny, sighing. " Women are your line. If only I'd known you then as well as I'm getting to know you now, you needn't have given any of them any more trouble."

"Ah, but this is different." The malicious smile caressed him shamelessly. "This is the love of a lifetime, my dear Truscott, and my intentions are honourable."

"Like all hell!" said Johnny.

They studied each other long and steadily.

"Think about it," said Chatrier, "think about it in the calm of solitude, my dear fellow, and I'm sure all your lame dogs can rely on you not to let them down by doing anything foolish."

Johnny looked at him for a long moment in considering silence, with nothing in his face to indicate either anger or uneasiness, and then without haste turned and walked out of the room, closing the door quietly behind him. There was no point in wasting energy in words or gestures now; thought was indeed indicated, and pretty urgently, too.

Even if Hero made a healthy recovery from her infatuation, this man would continue a potential danger to all those helpless people he had threatened. As long as he lived there was always the possibility that he might some day find it to his advantage to set the hunt in motion, for gain or for spite, or simply for sport if the fit took him.

Johnny happened to be down in Sam's box by the stage-door when Marc Chatrier came down from his dressing-room and strolled along the corridor to the door, where the car Johnny had put at his disposal was waiting for him. They watched him pass, hat at a debonair angle, whimsical mouth smiling faintly, eyes dreamily pleased with life and the sunlit noon. They did not take their eyes from him until the car slid forward from the kerb and vanished round the corner.

In the corner by the window Codger knitted away with silent devotion, his steel needles clicking merrily, his large eyes fixed fondly on Johnny. In his presence they never strayed.

"Marriage of Figaro!" said Johnny bitterly, staring after the acquisition he had hailed with such innocent pride not so long ago. "That fellow's ripe for a funeral, if everybody had what I wish him!"

CHAPTER THREE

JOHNNY CLOSED THE DOOR, and the faint, quivering, distant tremor of the strings leading into " *Porgi amor,*" one of the most melting sounds in the world, was cut off sharply, as if by a blow. The second act beginning, the house full and responsive, and the mysterious fine thread of splendid tension already lifting players and audience out of their everyday selves, into a world of superhuman achievement and supernormal sensitivity of apprehension; the two halves of a magic, making between them one of those miracles of a night that send human beings out renewed, never to be quite the same again. And Johnny shut the door on it with a clouded face.

" What's the matter? " said Gisela, turning from the glass. Marcellina's mantilla lay discarded on the ottoman by the wall, but she still wore the black lace dress with its tight, boned bodice of stiff silk. She had not the operatic figure; he could almost have shut her waist in his two hands. He tried it, smiling faintly as he stretched his long fingers; and all with that shadow still heavy on his eyes.

" Something's happened," said Gisela with certainty. " What is it? "

" Yes, something's happened, all right. Yesterday, after the rehearsal. I tried to get you on the phone afterwards, but you were out. And I didn't have time to speak to you alone before the curtain went up to-night."

" I knew there was something, or you'd have been in your box." Gisela swept Marcellina's lace gloves from the long stool before her mirror, and drew him down there beside her. " Tell me."

He told her, as simply and bluntly as if he had been confiding in a man. She listened in silence, her eyes intent upon his face. The shadow that lay upon him communicated itself to her. At the end she said, slowly feeling her way back through the years to a time she had often been adjured not to remember: " You say you took him aboard there in Italy ? Are you sure of him ? "

" Yes, now I am. Ever since he came I've had an uneasy feeling at the back of my mind that I'd seen him somewhere before, that I ought to know him. But from photographs I did know him—who doesn't ?—and I put it down to that. But as soon as he mentioned that trip I had him. I'm quite sure."

" Then he really does know about two people, at least. *Could* he make trouble for them ? After all this time, would anyone want to follow it up, even if they did get in with faked papers ? "

" I think they still might. I think so. *She*'d probably be all right, she's getting old, and she lives in retirement, they've never had any trouble with her. But the professor has one of those consciences you can't shut up. He's up to the eyes in nuclear disarmament, and you know how popular that would make him. It's taken his friends all their time as it is to keep him out of the active group and jail. And even if he was behaving like an orthodox lamb," said Johnny, ploughing deep furrows through his thick brown hair, "government departments don't like being by-passed. They're only too well aware that three parts of 'em are useless as it is, it doesn't pay to rub it in."

" So he must not set the machinery in motion," she said, " whatever happens."

" No, he mustn't. I could put up a good running fight over my own record, if it came to it, but I couldn't protect them. And now we know what cards he holds, it seems to me he'll always be a danger. Even if I did stand out of his way and give him a free hand with Butch—and I'll see him in hell first—I should never feel safe from him. The first time he chose to feel himself cramped, and start angling for some new concession, out would come the same threat. I could start an inquiry into his own record, and there might well be stuff there that would shut his mouth tight enough if we could get at it, but that's going to take time. It isn't even a question of Hero so much now," he said, scrubbing anxiously at his forehead. " I saw that as soon as the cards were down. He's served me with notice that he reckons he can do as he likes round here, or else. And a set-up like we've got here is a powerful attraction to a man whose voice isn't going to be getting any better from now on. I see a sort of dreamy look in his eye, as though he's seeing himself as director of productions here in a year or two. Can you think of a better old age pension for a man like him? "

" Open the door, Johnny," said Gisela. " You'll miss ' *Voi che sapete*.' "

He looked hastily at his watch and jumped to obey. To this room the sound from the stage came up faint but clear. Hero was already in full song; the notes soared light and true, pouring out all the agitation and ardour and haste of the boy in love with love.

Johnny stood with his head inclined, vulnerably fond and proud, smiling like an idiot, and Gisela, taking her eyes from him for a moment to stub out her cigarette, caught the same look on her own face, and smiled through her preoccupation.

" She's good, isn't she? " said Johnny, whispering, as shy as if he praised himself.

" She's *very* good, Johnny. And she'll be better yet, much better."

She waited until he had closed the door again on the busy voices of the Countess and Susanna, a faint, mingling murmur in which he was no longer vitally interested. Then she said: " It worries me, Johnny, about Hero. She has usually such a good instinct about men, how could she be taken in by him? Are you sure you're not mistaken? "

" I'm not sure of anything with her now," he admitted disconsolately. " I thought I knew her so well, and now she's got me baffled. But love does do funny things with very young girls—doesn't it? They go overboard for the most revolting specimens, you've seen it."

That was true enough; but still she frowned dubiously over this particular infatuation. " You know —it seems I must have been wrong, but I did think she was a little interested in Hans."

"*Hans?* " Johnny uttered a short howl of laughter. " I only wish she was. She hates the sight of him since his performance of two nights ago, even if she didn't before. Every time they come near each other now they're scrapping. Didn't you see them in the first act?"

His worried eyes gleamed momentarily at the memory.

" It's working out very well for the performance, as a matter of fact. I've never seen a *Figaro* where the Count and Cherubino really struck sparks from each other before. Gives it more body, you get the absurd rivalry between the jealous rooster and the chick, and at the same time a touch of reality in the heart of it, just the foretaste of a genuine rivalry to come, and no holds barred. It's taken his mind off Tonda and Inga, too, and that's all to the good. They were round his neck before, and much good that is, when they're supposed to be fighting him tooth and nail. Now their blood's up, and they're really tearing into him."

" I've noticed it," agreed Gisela dryly, and smiled with him for one pleased moment, warmed by his delight in his perfect plaything.

The first act had gone wonderfully; the spring was wound, and the play and counterplay of characters moved with a taut precision that fused them all into one reality and one conviction; and the music clothed the drama in a translucent splendour of sound that made it timeless and universal, transmuting the Count's autocratic tantrums, Cherubino's quivering romantic temerity, Figaro's sly, subversive fire, Susanna's shrewd, resourceful charm, all into the stuff of immortality. Franz, directing from the harpsichord, was incandescent with inspiration. Everything that happened on the stage seemed to emerge out of an inner certainty that possessed them all, like a dream in which you cannot put a foot wrong. Even when the Count, hauling Cherubino angrily out of the great chair, had dealt him a resounding slap on his neat satin behind to go with the thundered: " *Serpente!*" it had merely seemed to be an inspired improvisation arising inevitably out of his lordship's jealous frustration.

But hadn't it rather, thought Gisela, suddenly enlightened, been simply one opportunist blow in the off-stage battle those two were conducting, and nothing at all to do with da Ponte's libretto? A coincidental felicity! Maybe, after all, Johnny was worrying about nothing where Hero was concerned. Maybe!

There remained, however, the others. The problem was not resolved, and at the end of every flight they came back to Marc Chatrier.

" Yes," said Johnny, arriving by his own more circuitous route at the same insurmountable obstacle. She had taken up the black mantilla, and was arranging it carefully over her piled-up hair. He stood behind her, his eyes holding hers in the mirror, while he draped the folds over her shoulders. " Of course, I could kill him," he said thoughtfully.

" Don't talk such nonsense! " said Gisela fiercely. " Give me my gloves, it's nearly time I went down. And you'd much better come down with me and watch the performance."

Johnny smoothed out the long strands of lace, looking down at them with a closed and unrelenting face.

" But when you think," he said, " how many men we wiped out between us, just in the way of our daily work, not so long ago. Experts we were—had to be. And now we can't rub out a snake to prevent him from biting. Does it make sense? "

She took the gloves from him, stroking them on and rolling them up to her elbows. When it was done she took him by both hands, and he looked up into her face speculatively, keeping his own counsel.

"You won't have to do any killing," she said. "Whatever happens, neither you nor anyone you care for shall suffer at Marc Chatrier's hands. Don't worry about Hero, don't worry about the boys. You go and enjoy your triumph, and don't let anything spoil to-night for you. To-morrow's time enough for him."

Johnny stood mute for a moment, regarding her with a slightly rueful smile. Then he stooped his head impulsively and kissed her on the cheek.

"You're a great old girl, Marcellina. But you stay out of this, and leave the vermin-clearance to me. Come on, grab your contract and let's be after that lawyer of yours, or your husband will get away."

He checked suddenly in the act of towing her towards the door, turning on her a horrified face.

"Only suppose he really was your husband, girl! What a ghastly fate that would be!"

Before he left the bar, during the main interval, he stopped to have a word with Codger, who hovered greedy for his attention, struggling with the inevitable convulsion of all his disorganised features for speech.

Everybody made the extra effort for Codger. People who were in flaming tempers because of somebody else's idiocy or their own mistakes contained themselves and spoke gently and equably to their mascot. Even Franz, when everything went wrong at rehearsals and his language to his company outdid that of a drill sergeant handling an awkward squad, muted the explosions when Codger appeared within earshot.

"A new sweater, Codger! I never noticed." It was

a pleasant blue-grey this time. The welt was nearly finished, two inches of neat ribbing stood stiff on the bright blue plastic needles. Dolly always bought the wool for him; he couldn't manage the smallest such commission himself, though she sometimes took him with her to choose a colour, and no one ever objected if he selected a pastel pink or a luridly fashionable purple. "Did you finish the green one? Who's going to get this one when it's finished?"

Codger mouthed and gestured, agonising after the expression that always eluded him.

"It's for his lordship," translated Sam indulgently. "Took a liking to that lad, Codger has."

"Well, I'm sure it'll suit him," said Johnny loyally, "and look even handsomer than that satin waistcoat."

The effort to find something nice to say to Codger was always pathetically over-rewarded. He went away with Sam, beaming, satisfied with so little, understanding so little, so terrifyingly tenacious of what he did understand; and Johnny went to have a word with Hero before going round to his box for the third act.

He wasn't sure if she was still punishing him for turning into a heavy father at this late stage, so he tapped at the door with a not entirely light-hearted parody of trepidation; but the reluctant officer, very trim in her laced coat and white breeches, looked round and grinned at him, too preoccupied with the business in hand to remember any incidental grudges.

"Hi, Butch!" said Johnny.

"Hi, skipper! How'm I doing?"

She was busy laying out the dress she had to wear over her male clothes half-way through the act, so that she could dive into it and be laced up in the shortest possible time.

"You're doing *fine*," he said fervently, and loped over impulsively to kiss her. She lent him her cheek amiably, and returned him a hasty hug, but apparently she hadn't so much as noticed that he'd been missing from his box all through the second act. He was so proud of her he could hardly speak without spilling over.

"I'm going to be a case for Freud by the end of this business," said Hero, pushing him off as the warning bell sounded. "You've no idea how complicated it is trying to be a girl pretending to be a boy pretending to be a girl. Isn't it *odd* how the type persists? Thank *goodness* the composer in *Ariadne* doesn't dress up as a woman! Wouldn't you think they'd let a 'breeches part' *be* a breeches part?"

"You *would* be a transvestist," said Johnny, and patted the seat of her smart regimentals and fled, somewhat cheered on one issue at least. She might be annoyed with him, but it didn't go very deep. They could get back on to their old terms, if only the stumbling-stone could be removed. Removed. It had an easy, as well as a final, sound; but the word had no magic, and Marc Chatrier would not vanish for the sake of a wish.

Johnny watched the third act from his box. The complicated plot unfolded with a galloping impetus, so full of clichés, on the face of it, that it should have creaked at every turn, but so magically manipulated on the dazzling stream of the music that its very banalities illuminated the deepest places of the human heart, and the puppets blazed into a life more intense than realism

could ever have given them. Marvellously still, the
crowded house was uplifted and held taut on the tension
of the ravishing sound.

Susanna pretended surrender, the Count swung in a
few moments from triumph to frustrated malevolence,
and his hoped-for vengeance melted and slipped
through his fingers in the absurdities of the sextet, a
whole novelette in itself. Long-lost son and long-
bereaved mother (unmarried) embraced each other.

That cost Johnny his single lurching fall out of the
alchemy of Mozart into the reality of his own predica-
ment, the sight of Gisela and Marc Chatrier locked in
each other's arms. The sudden furious ache of his anger
astonished him. She ought not to have to touch the
fellow. And yet it was doubtful if at that moment she
was even aware of him except as Figaro, for they had
achieved the rare and timeless miracle, and they were
no longer players, but the very creatures of Almaviva's
castle of Aguas Frescas, near Seville, acting out their
immortal day unaware of being watched or overheard.

And there went Cherubino, the infant officer, slipping
across the stage hand-in-hand with the gardener's
daughter to hide himself among the village girls. And
here came the Countess, tall and pale and noble and
distressed, to dictate to her maid the letter that should
bring her jealous husband headlong into a trap.

Then the village girls bringing their flowers to the
Countess, and the shy country cousin, gawky under his
unaccustomed skirts—modern play-clothes made for
good Cherubinos—was first favoured and then un-
masked and scolded. And how little effect it ever had
on him! Young Nan Morgan, who played Barbarina,
took a deep breath and poured out her plea for him in

a piping flood, innocently blackmailing the Count into letting him off yet again.

And then the procession of the two wedding couples, with that splendid, stylish march. How had one man managed to draw up out of the well of sound so many superlative tunes? And how was it there were any left for later genius to find? You'd have thought Mozart had taken them all. Tunes that seemed to glide so lightly over the dimpling face of human experience, and yet pierced so deeply into the unfathomable places of the personality, far beyond anywhere the loud, portentous boys could reach, as lofty and as deep and as far-ranging as the spirit has room at its largest.

Her uncle the gardener led Susanna to kneel before the Count and receive her wedding veil from him. Figaro brought in his mother Marcellina to receive the same favour at the hands of the Countess. The march paraded all its bravery and gaiety as they crossed the stage hand - in - hand, Gisela's lace skirts swaying majestically about her.

They entered from the side opposite to Johnny's box, and he had their faces in full view and an excellent light. They smiled, the lightly linked hands were easy. But he saw their lips moving, very slightly and carefully and coldly.

He reached for the glasses in the pocket under the rim of the box; ordinarily he seldom used them. The smiling mask of Gisela's face leaped at him. It was a long time since he'd done any lip-reading, and the performance of professionals is a very different matter from the open speech of unsuspecting people; but he still had the accomplishment, one of many he had acquired for deadly purposes during the war. He watched, and read as best he could, missing words where there was not enough movement to give him a hold. He saw, framed almost imperceptibly on Gisela's lips, his own name.

"—touch Johnny," she said.

Chatrier was harder. His head was turned towards her, so that Johnny got only a partial view, but he saw the shape of "prevent me?" and then, strangely, with every implication of astonishing intimacy: "—my dear!"

" I've warned you," said Gisela clearly, and hand in hand with him she swung to face the Countess's chair. The last glimpse Johnny caught said distinctly: " You won't live to hurt him."

Marcellina sank to her knees, with a deliberation nicely distinguished from Susanna's lissome youthfulness, before the Countess. Figaro stepped back from her to his place beside his own bride, and the girls burst into their song of praise to their lord and master the Count. The mad day of Aguas Frescas drew to its climax and the end of the third act.

Johnny closed the glasses and put them away. The hand that snapped the catch of the pocket was not quite steady.

Figaro held the stage alone, the darkened stage shadowy with trees, the dim shapes of the two arbours discreetly withdrawn to left and right. He had set the scene for his revenge on the whole race of women, his witnesses were planted, his reproaches already prepared. He sang his raging aria with a contained but formidable passion that ripped the livery from his manhood. How could so small a spirit control so great a gift? On the bitter last line he withdrew into the stage pine-grove, gradually melting into the darkness until he vanished utterly from sight.

They were using a slightly cut version which omitted Basilio's aria, and transposed to this spot Barbarina's giddy little recitative about the supper she had begged for her hidden Cherubino.

" I had to pay for this with a kiss—but never mind, someone else will pay it back! "

The girl was going to be good, the secret fire of the evening had kindled a small flame in her, too. She heard the approach of Susanna and the Countess, and scuttled into the left-hand arbour with a tiny squeak of alarm. Oh, those arbours, stock properties of comedy like modern bedroom doors, tumbling out unexpected bodies at the end to confound everyone! Who would ever expect, if you wrote down the ingredients in cold blood, that something so transcendent could be made of them?

Barbarina had vanished, and the small conspiracy of women appeared, the Countess, Susanna and Marcellina all bound together by women's enforced loyalty to one another in face of the stupidity and unreason of men. They knew all about the invisible listener, and two of them sweetly withdrew to leave the third to pay out her lover for his suspicions by twisting the screw another turn or two. Marcellina followed Barbarina into the left-hand arbour, the Countess slipped away into the trees.

" ' Now we shall see the great moment,' " sang Figaro savagely out of the darkness; and again, echoing Susanna's demure teasing with aching ferocity: " ' To take the air—to take the air! ' "

Time had brought them full circle from the moment when Chatrier first came in. Johnny's mind, suddenly harking back to that hopeful entrance, recoiled in unreasonable revulsion from "*Deh vieni non tardar*." Tonda's voice was as limpid as spring water; she stood with the whole stage to herself, her pretty head thrown back, her round throat shaping and spilling the heavenly notes like floating pearls. Johnny drew back from her, and slipped away out of his box without a sound.

Perhaps the greatest love song ever written for a woman sank to its close in triumphant stillness, like a folding of wings. The dove settled and nestled, soft as down:

"'*Ti vo la fronte incoronar—incoronar—di rose.*'"

The whispering postlude followed on her heels as she drew back into the trees, dwindling like a candle-flame withdrawing into the night. Then, just as Figaro should have hissed his: "*Perfida!*" just as Cherubino tripped out of the wings with the trill poised on his lips, and the Countess moved softly forward from the bushes, Tonda hit a high note that was not in the score, the high note to end all high notes, soaring like a dart vertically to the roof of the theatre and sheering through it to split the night.

Cherubino, in the middle of a flushed and flustered entrance, jumped as though the steely point of that sound had pierced his flesh. The Countess dropped her handkerchief and swung about with an audible gasp. Faces loomed in the wings. The audience rustled uneasily and clutched at one another. And Tonda, drawing breath in a long, heaving cry, screamed and screamed until Franz signalled frantically from the orchestra pit, and the curtain came down between two uproars.

The stage lights went up, glaring white as the whole cast came running. Tonda was in a whimpering heap on the boards, her hands clutching her cheeks, her eyes staring in horrified shock at the body of Figaro, flat on his face among the stage trees with a pretty little dress rapier upright and quivering in his back.

CHAPTER FOUR

" Yes," said Hero, " I do recognise it, of course. It's mine. I don't mean just that I had to wear it in the opera. I had, but also it belongs to me. My father bought it for me once in Salzburg. It was made for a minor princeling, I forget his name, but he was thirteen years old, I remember that. I knew it was a real sword, not a toy."

She stood before Inspector Musgrave sturdily, her pale face fixed and resolute, her grey eyes flickering from his deceptively mild regard to the note-book on his knee. A grey, precise man of about fifty, in a dinner-jacket. Light-lashed eyes slightly magnified behind thick lenses, sharp, irritable features that suggested an experienced and intolerant law clerk rather than a policeman. But the thick, self-assured body in its good clothes indicated something rather more prosperous, perhaps an autocratic but on the whole benevolent company director out for an evening at the opera.

It was for a doctor Johnny had appealed, he hadn't bargained for a detective-inspector as well. Who would expect to find a Scotland Yard officer in the third row of the stalls ?

Musgrave's right hand was busily drawing and writing all the time he questioned; she could see the layout of the last act briefly sketched upon the page, and a lot of dots distributed about it. A dot which must be Tonda in mid-stage. A dot which could only be Inga in the dimness of the trees close to the right-hand arbour. An X which was the dead man, here where he had fallen. Hero looked down at the empty place on the boards from which they had removed the body after the photographers and the surgeon had done with it. There was a small, irregularly-shaped stain of blood there now to mark the spot. But so little! Who would think a man could die and leave so little trace?

" And you were supposed to be wearing it as part of your costume," said Musgrave. " I saw it, of course. You had it on when you ran through the hall with Barbarina in the third act. Then you made your next appearance with a dress over your uniform. Did you wear the sword then? "

" No," said Hero. " It's a nuisance under the petti-coats, you know."

He placed a tiny circle carefully in the wings on his plan, and wrote two names against it: Max Forrester and Ralph Howell. Together, so they said, at the moment when the alarm was given. And in the wings on the other side, ready for his impending entrance, the Count, this young Austrian Selverer. And here, close to Forrester and Howell, the girl, just tripping forward on to the stage, a shade flushed, a shade flustered—and without her pretty little smallsword.

" I see. And when did you last see it, then? You didn't have it during the fourth act, did you? "

" Well—I did. But then I . . ." She drew breath and swallowed the unsatisfactory opening to start again. " I meant to wear it again in the fourth act, and I actually put it on. But then I—the baldric broke. While I was still off-stage, that is. I . . . it was broken in an altercation."

The word had a triumphantly legal sound about it, she didn't know from what recess of her mind she'd dredged it in this emergency.

" Oh? " said Musgrave mildly. " An altercation with whom? "

" With Mr. Chatrier," she said in a hurried gasp.

Young Hans Selverer had been slowly and stealthily inching his way round the circle of tense and watchful people towards her, but at this he stood frozen, watching her across the few yards of intervening air with a heavy, anxious frown.

Musgrave had looked up from his labours sharply. Points of light gleamed behind his disguising glasses, and made him look less mild.

" You mean you were actually involved in some sort of struggle with him? " He had the scabbard across his knees, he handled it delicately through a handkerchief, lifting the frayed end of the rainbow ribbon. It had broken, apparently, in front, where it would cross her breast, and what was particularly notable about it was that the shorter end thus left, perhaps eight inches of it, had been torn away from its moorings. Only a few floating threads coiled and fluttered round the silver trappings of the scabbard at the front fastening. The length of ribbon was clean gone. The other end, long enough to span her slender back and reach down to her breast, was still firmly anchored to its silver buckle.

" This wouldn't take much force to break it, I realise that. But it can't have been ready to part of itself, all the same. What happened to break it? *Were* you struggling with him? "

" Yes," said Hero faintly.

" Please," said Hans, reaching her half a second

ahead of Johnny, and supporting her with a large young arm, " do not make her——"

" Butch," said Johnny anxiously, hemming her in on the other side, " do you know what you're saying? If he accosted you, why didn't you come to me? I . . ."

She shook them both off gently but firmly, and stepped a pace nearer to Musgrave, who had waited and watched with interest during this brief interlude. " I'm all right, really I am. Why shouldn't I be? And I *want* to tell him."

" A very sensible attitude," said Musgrave, inserting the dot which represented Marcellina, cosily in the left-hand arbour with the young one, that Nan child who played Barbarina. Two together again, lucky for them. He cast one glance at Gisela, who sat with folded hands on the property marble bench at the edge of the circle, patient and self-contained, her dark eyes ranging with quick intelligence from face to face.

" What was this altercation of yours about? " he asked, flashing back to Hero. " A commonplace amorous assault? " In a brief interval in her father's theatre it seemed hardly likely. He said so. Hero hesitated, her pallor suddenly flushed.

" Well, it's partly my fault. To some extent I—I suppose I'd been leading him on."

" Butch," said Johnny hastily, " that's making too much of it. You know there was nothing to it. You haven't, I suppose," he said hopefully, turning upon Musgrave, " got any just-grown-up daughters, have you? Pity! You'd know what it's like if you had. All she did to encourage him was have lunch with him a couple of times, and accept one dinner invitation. If I hadn't been a shade over-anxious she wouldn't even have thought of it as leading him on. Ridiculous phrase to use!"

"I see. You just had dinner with him once."

"Well, I didn't, actually. I meant to, but . . ."

She didn't know how to get round that incident, and before she knew where she was it was out. Better from her, perhaps, than from the staff of the Grand Eden. She thought of that, and took heart to tell almost the whole of it; and probably what she didn't tell Musgrave guessed for himself.

"Mr. Selverer happened to have to telephone my father over something, and he mentioned that I was there in the hotel, and my father asked him to drive me home at once. And he did," said Hero, simplifying somewhat drastically.

He didn't question it. He looked down critically at his drawing, and said mildly: "So Chatrier had some grounds for feeling encouraged. And to-day he presumed a little too far on your goodwill. When did this scuffle take place, and where?"

"It was in the corridor outside my dressing-room, not long before—before he was killed. It was while Gisela was singing that aria of Marcellina's. You know, when Figaro has rushed off threatening vengeance, and his mother says she'll warn Susanna, because women must stick together—and then she has that quite long aria——"

"I'm very well acquainted with the opera, thank you. I know the place you mean. So he had only just come off-stage, and you were coming from your dressing-room, all ready for your entrance in the middle of the act."

"Yes, but I had loads of time. I met him in the

corridor, and he—he wanted me to stop and talk to him, and I didn't want to. And—I pushed him off and broke away, and he grabbed the baldric and it broke. So I just ran back into my dressing-room and left him holding it. I locked the door, because I knew he had to go on again in a few minutes, before I did, so I only had to wait. He tried to coax me out, and then I heard him drop the rapier outside my door and go away."

" Did you open the door and take in the sword? "

" No, I waited several minutes to make sure he'd gone. I wasn't in any hurry. And when I did open the door there wasn't any rapier or baldric there, it was clean gone."

" Had you heard anyone pass during the interval? Anyone who might have taken it? "

" I didn't notice. There are often people about, naturally, but I wasn't paying any special attention. I wasn't listening, if that's what you mean, because I knew he had to go on, it was only a matter of waiting a few minutes. I . . ." This time she flushed darkly. " I had another go at my make-up, it was slightly mussed."

" So the sword was gone. And you didn't see it again? Not until it turned up in these—peculiar circumstances?"

" No, I didn't."

" And you haven't any idea who could have taken it from outside your door? "

" No, not the least idea."

Musgrave carefully spiced his plan with a few question marks which indicated the probable positions of supernumeraries like Sam Priddy. He looked up at Johnny with a strictly controlled smile.

" It seems you were wise to feel some misgivings about your daughter's association with the dead man, Mr. Truscott. May I take it that you didn't like Chatrier? Or was it merely a matter of his age? I quite understand that Miss Truscott may attract admirers who are not invariably—disinterested, shall we say? "

" I didn't like him," said Johnny firmly. It would appear in any case, better from him than from others. " I had reason to think that he saw my girl as a fortune, and my attitude towards him was what you surely might expect it to be. Professionally I had no quarrel with him. He was a splendid artist."

Undoubtedly, thought Musgrave, eyeing him steadily, this was not a man who would need any help in managing his own affairs in the ordinary way, without resorting to such extremes as murder. The young fellow was more likely to be pushed hard by his jealousy of an older man who had apparently been shown some favours. All the same, daughters can be the devil, and it was always possible . . .

Musgrave added a small, neat mark of interrogation to the wandering dot representing Johnny, an infinitesimal drawing of a man in orbit between his stage box and the wings. Hans Selverer already had his own question mark. The waiters at the Grand Eden would be able to fill in some necessary details.

" Well, I think I now have an idea of everybody's movements during the material time. What's remarkable is that we have such a short period to fill in. The last time anyone can be certain they saw or heard Chatrier alive was when he sang the final: '*Il fresco— il fresco!* ' during Susanna's short dialogue with the Countess, before '*Deh vieni.*' By the time Susanna

withdrew into the trees at the end of that aria he was
dead—or at least the attack that killed him had already
been made. A matter of no more than ten minutes.
With a brisker tempo it wouldn't have been so long."

" You found my tempo too slow?" said Franz,
bristling. " You want Susanna should gallop through
'*Deh vieni*,' and there should be no sudden catch in the
breath in the middle of all the horse-play? You will
teach me to conduct *Figaro* like I could teach you to
catch murderers."

" I don't wish to be unduly critical. I could quote
excellent authorities." For the first time the mild eyes
really took fire; it seemed the man had a passion, and
his ticket hadn't been a gift from a missionary friend,
or a concession to an aspiring wife. " I may say I was
very surprised," he said belligerently, " to see that a
cut version of *Figaro* was being used in *this* theatre."

" Cut," said Johnny, catching the spark, " at my
wish, and not to save time, either. Cut, and all the better
for it." His voice said plainly: " Want to make something of it?"

" To take out the 'ass's skin' aria—a very fine
aria——"

" Hear, hear!" murmured Ralph Howell tenderly
from the background. " And the only one Basilio has
to himself, mind you, bach!"

" A very fine aria," snapped Johnny, " and nothing
whatever to do with the business of the act. We axe
it because I prefer it that way dramatically, and trans-
pose Barbarina's recitative to that spot because it makes
the timing smoother. We never cut anything for any
reason except to get a heightened tension."

" We've got that, all right," said Forrester dryly,

shooting a modern wrist-watch from under Doctor Bartolo's great laced cuff. " Two in the morning, and we have to go from murder to musical criticism. What I want to know is, when can we at least send these girls off home to bed? "

" Very shortly now." Musgrave recovered the thread of business hastily. What would the local inspector think of him? And after accepting his prior presence so mildly and amenably, too. " If no one has anything to add to these provisional statements, I think we might let the ladies go."

He looked round the circle of feminine faces, brightening with the hope of release, losing the betraying lines of tiredness. The local man, who had said little during the interrogation, had fixed a thoughtful stare on the Countess, in whose pale blue Scandinavian eyes showed a gleam of purpose which held a certain promise.

" Miss Iversen, you wanted to add something? "

The sergeant poised his pencil hopefully. Inga looked out of the corner of her eye at Hero. Cherubino's sky-blue sleeve nestled gratefully into Hans Selverer's glittering brocade side, and his fingers clasped the boy-girl's elbow firmly and protectively. There had been a little too much of the boy-girl, but Inga was no longer deceived.

" I wait," she announced clearly, " for Miss Truscott to correct her statement, but she does not do so. I am a truthful person. I ask myself, what must I do? "

Herself, apparently, was ready and waiting with the answer.

" This I do not mention earlier, because I do not at first realise it is important. But I was a witness of this

—altercation between Miss Truscott and another
person. I regret, I much regret, she makes it necessary
for me to tell it, but it was not Marc Chatrier who broke
the ribbon of her sword."

She savoured her moment, the dismay in the grey
eyes that were alone eloquent in Hero's wooden face,
the flare of anxiety and apprehension in Johnny's.

" It was Mr. Selverer," said Inga with intense
satisfaction.

The hum and vibration of suppressed excitement,
shaking them all, sent the blood coursing up into the
Count's ingenuous face, and tightened his fingers upon
Hero's trembling arm.

" You saw them? " said Johnny, bristling. " Where
were you, then? "

" I happened to cross the corridor, coming from my
dressing-room . . ."

Tonda emitted an explosive snort of laughter. " Do
not believe her. She is jealous because the little one here
puts her nose out of joint with him. She will say anything, that one."

" You are calling me a liar, *madam*? " Inga's icy
claws came out; the northern lights spat and flickered
in her eyes.

Tonda bounced up from her chair joyfully. " Yes, I
say it! Worse than that you would do to pay her for
being so young, after all the fury you have put into
chasing him all in vain——"

" And you? " shrieked Inga. " You Italian washer-
woman with skirts kilted up to run after him faster—
you dare talk of chasing him? *You?* "

" Me, I do not pretend. I amuse myself, but if I lose

I lose, there are plenty of men. For you perhaps he was the last hope."

Johnny took Tonda about the waist just in time, Ralph Howell and Max Forrester closed in from either side upon Inga, and bloodshed was averted by the length of a finger-nail. The Countess, freezing into dignity again, brushed off the restraining hands, composed her maid's muslin skirts about her, and said with deadly simplicity:

" Ask her."

All eyes came back to Hero, who had grown paler by fierce degrees as Hans Selverer had grown redder.

" All right," said Hero with resignation, " it was Hans. But all the rest of it was true. I only altered the identity of the man."

" Only! " said Johnny in a frantic whisper meant for the ears of a higher providence. " My God, women! "

" Well, what's so surprising about that? " said Hero, goaded. " What harm could it do Marc Chatrier now, my saying it was him? After all, we're a company, we don't go round throwing suspicion on one another——"

" *Some* of us do not," snorted Tonda.

"—and it couldn't hurt him, so I made it him."

" So you thought," said Musgrave, " that Mr. Selverer might have made use of your sword, once he had it, to kill Chatrier, and you set out to divert suspicion from him."

" Of course not! I *knew* he didn't. In the first place he wouldn't, and in the second place I keep telling you he didn't take the thing away with him, he left it outside my door. But I thought *you*'d start thinking he'd done it."

" Couldn't you trust the police not to jump to conclusions quite so easily? "

" No," said Hero simply.

She caught her father's speaking eye, and protested indignantly: " Well, *do* people? Ever? You don't suppose he's got as far as being an inspector without knowing that, do you? "

Musgrave crossed out the two question marks with which he had flanked the dot which was Cherubino. They were no longer appropriate; she was too devastatingly reasonable to be associated with such equivocal symbols.

" Then I'm to take it, am I, that you would always lie for your friends if you thought it necessary? Even on oath? "

That made her face solemn for a moment. She thought about it, pulling at the curls of her wig, and then she said: " That would make it a bit dicey. But yes, I suppose so. If I was sure they hadn't done anything wrong. Wouldn't you? "

Don't answer that, Musgrave! Plead the fifth amendment if necessary, but don't answer it.

" Then how am I supposed ever to trust anything you say? How am I to tell the difference when you tell me something true? "

" I don't know," she owned. " That's a sort of occupational hazard, isn't it? Maybe I might look less sure of myself when I wasn't telling the truth—or maybe more, to compensate? It's hard to say."

He resisted the temptation to pursue this unexpected philosophical by-way, and got back to the matter in hand. " Well, suppose you tell me the truth now, and see if I recognise it."

" It happened just like I've told you, and just at the time I told you, only it was Hans. We'd been quarrelling, rather—most of the evening. About my being spoiled and selfish, and his being bossy and priggish. We were still at it then, and I'd had enough, and he wanted to make me listen to him, that's all. He grabbed the baldric, and it broke, and I ran off and locked myself in. He tried to get me to talk to him, and when I wouldn't he said, oh, very well, he'd leave the rapier propped up in the doorway for me. And he did."

She was emphatic on that point; she wanted him to have no doubts of her truthfulness this time. But there remained the doubt which she herself had raised: when lying, would she be more or less convincing?

" How do you know he didn't take it away with him, after all ? "

" Because it fell down after he'd gone. I heard the point of the scabbard slither on the polished floor, and then the hilt clattered on the boards. It must have rolled half across the corridor."

A nice detail, but one she had not mentioned before; that might be mere chance, for the point was a small one, but there was no doubt she was quick at picking her way through thorns.

He turned his attention to Hans, whose angry colour had not yet subsided.

" Mr. Selverer, do you wish to support this version ?"

" It is true," said Hans, and restrained himself from adding: " this time."

" Why did you not correct the previous one ? "

" Oh, don't be silly! " cried Hero reproachfully. " How could he, when I'd just told it in front of everybody? He never had a chance."

To everyone's surprise, Hans shook her sharply by the arm, and said in a tone Johnny found himself envying: "Be quiet! You have made quite enough trouble for everybody." More surprisingly still, she said: "I know! Sorry!" in a meek tone, and was quiet.

"Did you leave the sword there, as she says?"

"I did."

"And you didn't see it again until after Chatrier was dead?"

"No, I did not."

And yet they could still be in collusion. One story had fallen down because of the accident of Inga's intervention, they palmed another one with all the dexterity of old hands.

"Did you get on well with Chatrier, Mr. Selverer?"

"I respected his gifts and his knowledge," said Hans stiffly. "Working with him was not easy, but it was rewarding. As a man I did not care for him so much."

"But Miss Truscott did?"

"As Miss Truscott's father," said Johnny peremptorily, "I strongly object to that question. And if you've finished with her now I'd like to send her home."

Musgrave smiled, cocking an eyebrow at his colleague. "Very well, I think we can let all the ladies go now."

Marcellina, the quiet one, rose with a quick, reassuring look at Johnny Truscott, and he nodded at her gratefully, committing his troublesome daughter to her care without a word.

Hero kissed her father. "'*Pace, pace, mio dolce tesoro!*'" she whispered placatingly in his ear, and went off stumbling and yawning to take off Cherubino's finery.

Once he was in the theatre, there was no way of getting him out. Wherever they turned, in the store among the sets, in the wardrobe, in the dressing-rooms, round the switchboard, down in the orchestra pit, there Musgrave would turn up, silent, still, and unbelievably obtrusive. The local man, though he took over the official business of statements and interviews, seemed to be able to go and come without creating those pregnant silences round about him, or drawing the deck crew prowling on his heels. The sergeant and his underlings who did the routine work of searching dressing-rooms and watching the comings and goings of the company were ordinary human beings, with whom casual communication was possible. But Musgrave did not so much visit the theatre as haunt it.

"That man's just about had this place to pieces already," said Dolly Glazier, polishing glasses in the circle bar before the evening performance of *Alceste*, three nights after the catastrophe of *Figaro*. There had been no pause in the activities of the Leander Theatre; one morning rehearsal had been cancelled to allow the exhausted Franz to sleep late, but that had been the only concession. "We're a commercial undertaking," Johnny had said, magnificently if not strictly truthfully, " and we keep faith with the public." *Arabella* had gone on according to plan on the night after the tragedy, and *Don Giovanni* the next night, with every man on his mettle. "What's he after now," said Dolly, "that's what I want to know."

"Keeping an eye on the lot of us," said Sam.

" Thinks if he hangs around long enough, somebody's going to lose his nerve and give himself away."

" But what's he looking for, anyhow? "

" A bit o' ribbon," said the old man, soft-voiced, " off our kid's sword-belt. That's my guess, anyhow. That's the only thing that went missing. Drop it in the furnace if you find it, girl, that's what I say."

" Destroying evidence! " said Dolly reprovingly. " Not that I'd go a step out of my way to help round up the one who knocked off that Chatrier fellow, that's a fact. I don't believe it was any of Johnny's folks, mind you. But it's a bit too close for comfort, all the same."

" I wouldn't mind," said Stoker Bates heatedly, " if he'd stick to detecting, but he don't. Takes on to learn me to scene-shift—me! Tells the old geyser how to conduct, very nearly. The other day, when Jimmy the One was in, blow me if this chap wasn't telling him what was wrong with the casting, and who he should have signed up instead of half the company. And you know what? . . . He thinks Wagner's better than Mozart! "

" *No!* " gasped Dolly, scandalised.

" True as I'm standing here. I heard 'em at it yesterday. Mozart, he says—*Figaro*, he says—*pleasant enough pastiche*, he says. Now *Tristan*. . . . Teutonic bluster, says Johnny. Not that he means it, not really, but what can you do with a bloke like that? *Pastiche!* "

They looked at one another in mute decision, writing off Musgrave from that moment. A policeman has his job to do, they could have forgiven him that; even his unnerving ways of erupting under their feet were perhaps only the symptoms of an occupational disease.

But a man who could prefer Wagner to Mozart was beyond the pale.

"He's here again," said Sam, putting his head in at Johnny's office door on the sixth morning after the final exit of *Figaro*. "Siegfried without his helmet! Wants to see the maestro, he says. Right now he's busy lousing up the piano rehearsal. I reckon if we don't get him up here out of Mr. Southall's hair pretty soon there's going to be more murder done."

"Damn!" said Johnny, and rose to switch off the tape recorder. They were playing through their two-year-old production of *Rosenkavalier*, in preparation for planning the new one to take pride of place in their next winter repertoire, and to call a halt in the middle of the rising excitement of Octavian's arrival, with the argument about Hero still far from settled, was frustrating, if not a kind of blasphemy. "Oh, well, must co-operate with the law, I suppose. Send him up."

Franz took his slippered feet off the desk, and fretted irritably at his silver mane. "I tell you the child can do it. If we can find her a Sophie who is young enough also, she can do it, and the work will gain."

"She isn't ready," repeated Johnny. "She says she isn't, and who am I to shove her into such a responsibility until she feels able to carry it?"

Gisela rose and shook together the preliminary drawings for the costumes. "I'd better leave you to it. Personally, I'd love to see an Octavian who really was still in his teens. What do you say, Sam?"

"Our kid?" said Sam, divining the cause of this mild dispute. He flicked a gesture of confidence at them with thumb and forefinger as he walked out. "Do it on her head," he said scornfully, and rolled away down the stairs with his ungainly but nimble gait.

Presently they heard Musgrave's deliberate feet ascending.

"No, don't go, Gisela," said Johnny, drawing her back as she would have made for the door with the portfolio of sketches. "Maybe he won't stay long."

"He seems to be practically a permanent resident," she said with a resigned smile; but she sat down again.

Musgrave came in brisk and large as ever, the slight expression of superiority provoked by Franz's belligerent deputy still on his precise features. He couldn't resist commenting. If he came with a warrant for me in his pocket, Johnny thought sourly, he'd still have to stop and tell us we were taking the second act finale too fast.

"You've put *Figaro* back into rehearsal, I see."

"It won't be out of the programmes more than a fortnight," said Johnny, pushing the cigarettes and the desk lighter towards him.

"Your substitute seemed to me to be doing very well."

"A lightweight," said Franz. "A small voice and no presence. He does his best, but it will be a travesty."

"Hm, I see Chatrier has at least one mourner."

He had not many, it seemed; his connections were professional only. A married sister in Colmar had written but not put in an appearance, and it had been left to his American agent to claim his body and set in motion the preparations for his funeral. But the musical critics of the world's Press, at least, were weeping ink for him by the column.

Musgrave settled his briefcase comfortably beside him, and leaned back in his chair.

"I won't keep you from your work long, Dr. Hassilt, but I think you may be able to help me. The international musical world isn't so big that artists of your calibre can revolve in it as long as you have without encountering most of the others of the same rank. And opera has always been your speciality. Tell me, did you ever hear of a baritone named Antoine Gallet? It would be some time ago, about the end of the war, or even during it."

Franz was regarding him narrowly from under knitted brows. "Yes, I have heard of him."

"Ever meet him?"

"Once, in Vienna, in 1942. He sang at one of the last concerts I conducted before I left Austria."

He had left it, like so many others, just ahead of the axe. It was a long time ago, and he never talked about it. Probably he seldom even thought about it. Music is a present world, perpetually renewed.

"I did not know him personally, apart from that."

"But you knew his reputation? It seems he was known as a collaborator. Born in Alsace, apparently, and he began to make extensive tours and to claw out a fairish living for himself after the Germans occupied France. Ditched his wife in the process, incidentally. They can't have been married more than a couple of years. Divorced her and let her be herded off to a concentration camp. And later he seems to have been responsible for several similar incidents. The records tend to be blank, so much having been destroyed. But rumour says he got several musicians into trouble while he was in Austria, including a certain conductor who ended up in Auschwitz. Died there, about a year later. Did you know all that about him? "

" Not the details, no. Certainly not about his wife. I knew he was looked upon as—pliable, and that he was quick to extricate himself from any association that might compromise his own safety. People were expendable. Every man for himself. He was young and he was frightened. Frightened people are not at their best."

" And did you know that he went to America after the war, changed his name—though he seems to have changed it once or twice already, for that matter—and made quite a new life and reputation? I think you did. You seem to have welcomed him," said Musgrave, pouncing happily, " when he came here in his new identity to sing Figaro for you."

Franz leaned forward, his irascible old face constrained to lines of laboured patience.

" *Meester* Musgrave," he said gently, " I am seventy-five years old. I no longer think I have the right to judge men and write them off for life, because in certain bad circumstances they have failed to behave like heroes. Gallet—that was twenty years ago, and what profit is it to harrow over it any more, if he is now another man? When Mr. Clash cables that he has signed up Marc Chatrier I am simply glad, because now I have the best Figaro now alive, and my job is to get as near perfection as a man can. If he deserves only good of me now, good he shall have——"

" And if not? " said Musgrave quickly. " How if he turned out to be the same even when he wasn't young and frightened? How if he began making hell all round him, for the people you like? "

" If he made trouble I could deal with him. I could protect my friends and colleagues."

" I see. He got the benefit of the doubt, though you knew he was Gallet. . . . You agree you did know that?"

" I knew it."

"—and if he made trouble, you would feel responsible for the security and peace of mind of your friends, and take steps accordingly."

" Such as with a sword, Franz, my boy," said Johnny bitterly. " Don't put words into my musical director's mouth, Mr. Musgrave, you've got two independent witnesses here if you do. Motives don't come much thinner than that."

Musgrave was smiling. " Thank you, Dr. Hassilt, that's really all I wanted. And now if I could just have a word with Mr. Selverer before I leave you——"

" I am going down," said Franz, ruffled and breathing hard, " I will ask Hans to come up to you."

" If you don't mind, I'd rather you stayed here."

An instant of sheer, uncomprehending surprise, and then Franz understood. He sat down again with a look of faint contempt, and Johnny, resigned, picked up the telephone.

" Stoker, my apologies to Mr. Southall, and would he mind asking Mr. Selverer to come up here for a few minutes."

Hans came up flushed and preoccupied from rehearsal, and checked sharply in the doorway at sight of Musgrave. In his presence all faces were guarded, he was used to that, and accomplished at reading even between the lines they smoothed away. The young man came in with eyes full of reserve, in a face held very still. He looked aside once at Gisela, and she smiled at him.

Was it imagination that the tension of his jaw and mouth eased a little?

" I'm sorry to take you away from rehearsal," said Musgrave with all his deceptive mildness flowing like honey. " This won't take a moment."

It sounded ominously like a dentist's reassurance before the pouncing extraction of a tooth, and that was much the way it turned out. The question came briskly and brightly this time, before the boy had even settled himself in a chair.

" Do you know the name Antoine Gallet, Mr. Selverer?"

Hans jerked up his head with a wild start that made an answer unnecessary. His hands gripped convulsively in the upholstery of his chair for a moment, and then with painful care relaxed their tension.

" Yes," he said.

" Ah, I thought you might. Did you ever see him? Or photographs of him, perhaps?"

" I never saw him in person. Photographs I may have seen, but I do not now recall it. It would be a very long time ago. Why do you ask me about him? Surely he is dead?"

Musgrave's particular smile, come and gone in an instant and leaving no ray behind, touched his grey countenance and fled. " Oh, yes—he's dead! Tell me what you remember hearing about him."

Hans moistened his lips, and pondered the wisdom of complying, though the look in his ingenuous eyes suggested pure bewilderment and mistrust rather than any personal disquiet.

" I know he was a singer who used to have a certain modest reputation during the war. I have heard my mother speak of him. But I have not heard the name now for many years."

"Yet you hadn't forgotten it. Well, it seems I'm better informed than you. He had another kind of reputation, too, for taking care of his own career by all manner of questionable tricks. There was a case, for instance, involving a conductor who was already suspected of anti-Nazi sympathies, and Gallet chose to bolster up his own position by refusing to work with this man, and getting him thrown out of his job, and finally he died in a concentration camp. His name, it turns out," said Musgrave deliberately, " was Selverer. Richard Selverer."

He looked up into fixed blue eyes that were staring at him in detestation. " A coincidence, would you say?"

" You know you are speaking of my father. If I did not choose to speak of this myself, it is because I did not and do not see what it has to do with you. I do not like this intrusion."

"You'll see the application very soon. When Antoine Gallet came here a little while ago to sing Figaro in this new production . . ."

Hans was on his feet, quivering. " What are you saying? I don't understand. Are you seriously trying to tell me that *Marc Chatrier* was Antoine Gallet? "

" My dear Selverer, are *you* seriously trying to tell *me* that you didn't know? "

" How could I know? I never saw him. I thought he was dead long ago, the name had vanished. It is only something I remember from a child. I never associated Chatrier with him. Why should I? "

" Ah, but you see, there was someone here who could very well have told you. Doctor Hassilt knew."

" I have told him nothing," said Franz flatly and coldly, " and you will certainly never prove that I did. Sit down, boy, sit down and calm yourself. The man is trying to get you to incriminate yourself, and so far, I must say, he is failing. But ludicrously! "

" And, for God's sake! " protested Johnny. " The boy must have been about seven years old. How tenacious do you think a child can be? "

" Oh, I'm not suggesting it's been on his mind all this time as a filial duty, not at all. But when the man unexpectedly turns up here in the person of this great man Chatrier, right here on the spot, rubbing shoulders with the son daily as he once did with the father—well, you see there could be a powerful compulsion there."

Hans sat down slowly, and let out his breath in a fierce sigh. " I think there could," he acknowledged grimly. " But I tell you again, until you just told me yourself, I had not the least idea that Chatrier was Antoine Gallet."

" That may or may not be true, we have only your word for it. But the background is suggestive. Then there is also this added element of your rivalry with Chatrier over Miss Truscott——"

" We are *not* rivals," protested Hans, flaming. " You have no right to speak so of Miss Truscott."

"—and there is the plain fact that you are the last person known to have handled the sword with which Chatrier was killed. Your prints are on both hilt and scabbard. The only other prints found on it are those of Miss Truscott and her father."

Hans frowned with distaste at the sturdy, well-shaped fingers which had supplied the sample prints to implicate him now more deeply. " I handled it, of course,"

he said. " But I left it there propped in Hero's doorway, just as she told you, and I did not see it again until
after the murder."

Gisela rose, crushing out her cigarette in the silver
ash-tray beside her chair, and came forward to the desk.
She had sat all this time in silence, only her eyes ranging
from face to face as they talked, and once at least
widening and flashing at Hans Selverer in what might
have been either a reassurance or a warning. Musgrave
had almost forgotten she was there; Marcellina was
always the quiet one. He looked up in surprise to find
her close at his elbow.

" I think," she said mildly, " it is time *I* said something, before you fall too deeply in love with the idea of
Mr. Selverer's guilt. No doubt you'll come to the
conclusion that all women are as unscrupulous as Hero
warned you. But I think that won't surprise you."

Hans was struggling to catch her eye, signalling
alarm and entreaty. She let her hand rest upon his
shoulder to hold him still and silent.

" He was not the last person known to have handled
the rapier, Mr. Musgrave. *I* picked it up in the
corridor that night. I'd forgotten my fan, and I went
back to my dressing-room to get it after I'd sung my
aria and made my exit. I have to pass Hero's door.
She told you the truth on one point, at least. The rapier
had slipped down and rolled into the corridor, and I
kicked it accidentally—those enormous skirts, you
know, one's feet tend to be unguided missiles. So I
picked it up and brought it down with me into the
wings."

" Your prints don't appear on it," said Musgrave,
almost indignantly.

" Chance is so inconsiderate, I am sorry. It's with no evil intent that Marcellina always wears long black lace gloves. I never even thought how useful they were being."

" And *why* did you pick it up in the first place? "

" It occurred to me suddenly," she said, looking him calmly in the eye and uttering the words without emphasis, " to kill Chatrier with it."

Johnny was on his feet, his hand gripping her arm. " Gisela, *shut up!* " He turned on Musgrave, who was staring intently, the deep inward gleam of the hunter in his eyes tempered by a certain wild distrust. " She's trying to confuse the issue to cover everyone else, that's all this is. What she says *can't* be true, you know that already. She was in the arbour with Nan before Chatrier was killed, and she didn't leave it until Tonda screamed and we all came running. You *know* that—you were there, too."

" I didn't say," protested Gisela reasonably, " that I killed him. I said I took the sword because I *thought* of killing him. Oh, no, I didn't *do* it." She put off Johnny's hand very gently from her arm.

" Then what did you do with the rapier? " demanded Musgrave.

" I propped it outside the left-hand arbour. When I went on-stage I had to hide in that arbour—but you know all the details of the libretto."

She smiled; he had told them so often enough.

" If Barbarina hadn't got bored and wandered off until the finale, as she very well could have done, I was going to send her to fetch something from my dressing-room. If she'd gone already, then the coast would have been clear for me without any trouble. Then I was

simply going to walk out at the back of the arbour, pick
up the rapier, and kill Figaro with it. In the darkness
of our stage forest it wouldn't have been difficult to
come up behind him—theoretically, at any rate. And
the rapier is a very fine piece of eighteenth-century
swordcraft, and extremely sharp, as you must know—
it's your Exhibit A. In practice, of course," she said, a
tremor convulsing her calm face for a moment, " I
expect I shouldn't even have found it possible when
it came to the point. It didn't arise, anyhow. Barbarina
was still there, and before I got rid of her I felt out at
the back of the arbour, where I'd propped my sword,
and it wasn't there. It hadn't fallen, or anything. It
was gone. So I just stayed there with Nan, and didn't
do anything deadly, after all. And I think I was glad."

" But if this is true," said Musgrave, thin and sharp,
" anyone could have taken the thing. Any one of you."

The case was wide open again. Selverer was still a
possibility, but not more so than any of the others who
darted about backstage in the fevered comings and
goings of that last act. And even Truscott himself—he
had been in his box just before Susanna embarked on
"*Deh vieni*," but he had certainly not been there by the
time she withdrew into the trees at the end of it. He'd
been prowling back and forth all through the performance like a lost soul.

" Well, not quite anyone," said Gisela. " I couldn't,
Nan couldn't, and Tonda couldn't. But it certainly
leaves it rather open."

Musgrave looked up at her in silence for a long
moment, and then asked the final, the inevitable
question. She was quite ready for it. The large eyes
stared back at him unwaveringly.

" Why? Because I could not tolerate that he should disrupt the lives of others as he once disrupted mine, and go on all his life ruining and hurting people. I don't suppose you followed up the record of his marriage far enough to find out his wife's maiden name? A mistake, Mr. Musgrave. As you said, the international musical world is not such a large one. She was also a singer from Alsace. Her name was Gisela Salberg."

For one instant of utter silence they stared at her and held their breath.

" She'd been very much in love with him," said Gisela, low-voiced. " You can imagine what it did to her, when he threw her to the wolves to save his own skin, and snatched back even his name from her. Yes," she said bitterly smiling, reading the mind that calculated frantically behind Musgrave's startled eyes, " isn't that a wonderful motive for murder? Better than the one you dug up against Hans, and far better than the one you were trying to foist on to Doctor Hassilt. What a pity, what a pity Nan was with me in the arbour every moment of the time! "

CHAPTER FIVE

MUSGRAVE CAME AND went by the stage-door these days, like a member of the company who had rights there; yet most unlike, for wherever he passed a slight chill followed, a stillness and a hush. Hands froze on what they were doing, voices dried up for a moment in contracted throats, heads turned stealthily, stiffly, trying not to be caught at it. He was like walking bad luck, the evil eye on two legs. Mateo, who was Maltese and not quite canny himself, actually marked a thumb-sign surreptitiously on his thigh as the alien went by.

Playing solo in Sam's box during their lunch hour, they felt him enter, and the cards hung suspended over the table until he had passed. Hero, sitting in with a hand while Stoker Bates shopped for his missus, looked up with the ace poised in her hand, and could not put it down until he had gone past the glass hatch and vanished. It was wrong, it was cruel; he wasn't even a bad fellow, and yet they all felt leagued against him, drawn into a solid phalanx of enmity as soon as he appeared. Why? Did they really believe one of their own people had killed Chatrier?

Yes, they did. They really believed it. She felt that intensely as she played her card and made her solo. Did they also have clearly conceived ideas about who the murderer could be? When she came to consider it, she was sure that they had; but they were hiding them even from themselves, and no two of them had quite the same theory.

Stoker Bates, by his more than usually protective attitude, favoured herself. She had never thought of it in that light before, and it caused a shudder of mingled horror and gratitude to run down her spine. They would love her even if she'd killed a man! They would close in round her more formidably than ever. Then was that why Sam was following Johnny about so faithfully, more than ever like a devoted guard-dog?

The shadow had withdrawn from them, and the silence went with him. Only Codger, who experienced their fears and forebodings dimly as a tremor of dread shaking his flesh, sat uncomprehending and mute knitting away industriously at Hans Selverer's blue-grey sweater, his large, confiding and yet unfathomable eyes fixed upon her. She was Johnny's; in the absence of Johnny himself she represented him, and Codger watched her jealously and lovingly, the sum and symbol of faithfulness.

" I thought we might be shut of *him*," said Mateo, dark eyes following the sound of Musgrave's feet along the corridor while his head never turned, " once the inquest was over."

" He hasn't found his bit o' ribbon yet," said Sam, shuffling the cards. " Likely he never will, and we shall have him running round grey-headed, give him time, like Lord Lovell looking for his bride. That isn't the way I like the ghost to walk. Your call, Chippy."

" *Is* the inquest over? " asked Hero, sorting her cards between her fingers with expert speed. " I thought they adjourned it."

" They did, love, for a week, but the week was up

yesterday. They brought it in murder against persons unknown, like you'd expect."

" And it *was* my sword that killed him? " Somehow at the back of her mind she'd always preserved a dream-like hope that it wouldn't be.

" There was a lot of technical bits about the wound, this wide and that deep, and such and such an angle, and how it penetrated the heart, and all that stuff. But yes, that's what it added up to. Why, what else were you thinking might have done it? "

" Oh, I don't know, I just thought you never *know*. I'd rather it hadn't been my sword. I don't think I want it back."

" You stop thinking too much about that and too little about the hand you're holding, or these thugs'll have the dress allowance out of your pocket. You got a winning streak if you keep your mind on it. Come on, now, call! "

" Abundance! " she said, rallying valiantly.

" Make it! "

She made it. It looked as if the wool fund, where her winnings invariably ended up, was going to be in pocket as a result of Stoker's shopping expedition. She had to take their money if she won, it was a matter of honour.

"Who d'you reckon *he* thinks done it?" asked Mateo, low-voiced, jerking his head after the enemy.

" I wish I knew. Mate, I only wish I knew."

" He'd like to think it was Miss Salberg, only he can't because the young 'un was with her the whole time. And he'd like to think it was Johnny, if he could prove Johnny knew about this bloke being the bastard who did the dirty on her years ago, but he can't. And he'd like to think it was the maestro, only he was tinkling the blooming continuo until the balloon went up. And he'd like to think it was his lordship the Count, only he didn't get the right sort of rise out of him when he sprang it on him Chatrier was this other fellow. Or any two of 'em or any three of 'em in conspiracy," said Chips morosely, collecting tricks with a large brown hand that was minus the upper joints of three fingers, " he's not fussy. And I'm not saying Johnny might not have felt like doing it, for that matter, *if* he'd known."

" Shut up about it," said Sam, drawing hard at his foul old briar, that gurgled and plopped like the crater of a small boiling geyser, " and deal the last hand. It'll have to be the last. You lot o' layabouts have got to get old Astro-what's-her-name's flying machine assembled before to-morrow morning's rehearsal, as well as three major shifts to-night. And it'd better work, too! Our Queen of the Night's in a bad enough temper already since she ain't been speaking to Miss Gennoni. If that thing drops her we've all had it! "

They played out the hand, and went off wrangling about the drop of the cards. Hero lingered still, sitting by Codger's side and stroking out the curling grey-blue sleeve that dangled from his needles. She talked to him softly and sadly, her heart not quite in it; and he made the low, loving, animal noises that were as near as he could get to speech.

She was watching the glass hatch and listening for the click of the stage-door opening.

Hans had hardly spoken to her for six days, and never once asked her to go out to lunch with him. He was kind and correct, and a little distant, and impossible to pin down; and she felt in her heart that she'd made a hash of it again, and made him dislike her for life. It seemed she could have had a gentle, sexless intimacy with him, and she hadn't been satisfied with that; and now all she'd got in its place was complete rejection. He just didn't like spoiled, self-willed girls. He'd take care of them if they'd got themselves into a spot, but not out of love or even liking, only because he was the conscientious sort. And be glad to drop them as soon as he could. Small blame to him, either.

Sam patted her shoulder, and said: " Stop fretting, kid, it can't go on for ever. Mr. Nosey Musgrave'll get tired and go away, just give him time."

" Sam," she said, letting her head rest gratefully against his hip, " Johnny couldn't really have done it, could he? "

" Who am I to say who could and who couldn't do things? We all could, very likely, if the chips happened to fall a certain way. But what's better than couldn't— Johnny didn't. You keep hold o' that, and never mind anything else."

" Oh, Sam! And it's all my fault, isn't it? I'm no good to Johnny, and I'd be no good . . ."

She didn't finish it, because she had caught back Hans Selverer's name in time; and she never heard Sam's indignant abuse and reassurance, because the click of the stage-door slamming open had brought her to her feet instantly, eyes brightening wistfully, ears pricked.

The step was the right step. She was out of the door and walking nonchalantly along the passage before Sam could blink away the dazzle of enlightenment.

" Oh, hallo! " said Hero brightly, slowing her step

and continuing to occupy almost the centre of the corridor, so that he should not be able to pass her politely, and speak briefly, and hurry on.

"Hallo!" said Hans perforce, curbing his pace to hers because there was no way of escape. The small, constrained frown did not leave his brow, but it shook for a moment, as though he would have liked to smile, and dared not. He was stiff and, she felt, wary. He kept his chin up and his eyes forward as though it might be dangerous to look at her. Taking no chances, she thought dolefully. But she tried her best.

"Have a nice lunch?"

She disliked that as soon as it was out; it sounded too much like a reproof for not asking her to join him. But what else was there neutral and safe to talk about while they went through the difficult approach steps? My God, what we've come to, she thought dismally; we even talk about the weather.

"Yes, thank you. And you?"

"Johnny had it brought in to-day, nobody can get him away from the sets for next year's *Rosenkavalier*. He's up there with Mr. Fawcett now, they've got all the little pieces out, moving and assembling them like kids with a toy train. They're nice!" said Hero, warming into a flush of hope and pleasure. "Would you like to go up and see them?"

"I would, of course—but—not now, perhaps. Franz wants me for just half an hour, and then I must go back into town. Perhaps to-morrow." His voice was careful and gentle, feeling its way painfully, trying not to hurt. He still did not look at her.

"But Franz is up there, too, he's as bad as Johnny.

He wants everything different. They always fight about sets."

They had reached the shadowy corner at the end of the corridor. She turned her face up to him gallantly, but the smile had never given her more trouble. His arm touched her breast inadvertently for an instant, and she felt him shrink from the contact.

" I—no, not now, Hero. Excuse me! "

She turned squarely to face him then, a faint flush of returning indignation colouring her cheeks.

" All right, I know. I'm sorry, I shouldn't have pushed you into having to say it. You don't want anything to do with me off-stage. I can understand it, but ... I just hoped ... I know it's all my fault," she said, " and I know what you think of me, but I thought at least we might try making the best of it. I *am* trying——"

" Hero," he said agitatedly, " you *don't* know! I *don't* blame you. How could you think——? "

He wrenched his head aside to break the compulsion his eyes felt to devour her too openly.

" To-morrow," he said desperately and not very coherently, and slipped past her and went up the stairs as fast as dignity would let him, and perhaps a little faster.

The sets for *Figaro* came out of store after a fort-night's banishment, and were assembled ready for the smooth transitions on which the deck crew of the *Hellespont* prided themselves.

Johnny prowled the wings from piece to piece, his eye all the time on Musgrave, who lurked in the orchestra pit, desultorily pulling the first act design to bits and reassembling it nearer to his heart's desire. He made no attempt to pass unnoticed, there was nothing stealthy about him; sometimes Johnny wondered if he really came in the hope of discovering anything new about the death of Marc Chatrier, or whether his monomania had fettered him for ever to the only opera house to which he had ever had completely free access. It was a nightmare thought, that they might have him for ever, the voice of something too extreme to be called criticism, something close to disintegration.

"—all that ring-o'-roses round the arm-chair, that's a pure comedy convention. You ruin it by all this realism —having an elaborate love-seat really big enough to hide in. It's too heavy-handed. And the realistically darkened pine-grove in the last act—all those *commedia del arte* characters in disguise don't really have to carry *conviction*."

"They do in this theatre," said Johnny, his pulses tingling again at the thought of the darkness in that pine-grove. But for that insistence on conviction Marc Chatrier would have been still alive. A little more light, and no one would have dared.

"You're taking Mozart out of his world."

"All worlds belonged to Mozart," said Johnny. "All inhabited worlds, anyhow. The word is universal. And you know what? ... That's why he vanished. His body couldn't be in one place. 'The dewdrop slips into the shining sea.' The lad's everywhere."

"I always understood that as meaning the loss of the dewdrop," said Musgrave with his faintly superior near-smile, threading his way between the angular, silent music-stands.

"You would!" said Johnny. "It's one of the funda-

mental divisions of humanity—like warm people and
cold people, and people who eat the top of their iced-
cake first and those who save it till last."

He was out of sight of his antagonist at that moment,
the defence in depth of the standing sets between them.
He stood under the arched entrance of the left-hand
arbour, where Nan and Gisela had retired that night of
the tragedy, and inadvertently given each other the
firmest alibi possible. A series of flat washes on canvas
under full light, a magic of branches and deep shadows
by stage lighting, and within, light or dark, this
framework of stiffened canvas and hessian on two-
by-four.

He moved deep into its recesses from the lecturing
voice that pursued him, his fingertips running
affectionately up and down the woodwork and dimpling
the fabric. Here at the back Gisela had reached out her
hand and felt for the sword. He still could not believe
in the strange events of that night, or rather his mind
believed in them but his senses could not adjust themselves to the idea of Gisela steeling herself, putting
out her gloved hand for the weapon she had laid
ready.

He repeated the gesture. Nothing. And then she
was free. She, but not the other person, the one who
had lifted the burden from her.

He drew back his hand. Close to his eyes as he
turned, wavering gently in a faint current of air, a
floating thread of red, fine as a hair, signalled from the
crevice between the wood and the canvas. A thread of
frayed silk, one strand from a thread, rather. He pulled
it, and it parted at a touch, clinging to his fingers
with the living vigour of silk. But short and bright, a

thicker end of blue followed it into the light, a down of white, the infinitesimally tiny corner of a scrap of material.

He inserted his fingertips very carefully, and felt along the folded edge of a small, flat thing wedged tightly between canvas and stay, close to where they were fastened together. The feel of the silk, vibrant, organic, tingled through the nerves of his hand, and set the hairs on his wrist erect. Folded in three, fine as gossamer, it took up very little room. He smoothed even the last delicate filament out of sight. He dared not do anything else; the didactic voice was drawing nearer, coming to look for him; Musgrave was out of the orchestra pit, and up on the stage.

Johnny went out to meet him, calm of face and empty of eye, went past him and stood in mid-stage looking round upon his assembled toys.

" The trouble with you, Musgrave," he said, " is that you've lost the capacity for honest, generous delight, and because you can't enjoy it you're damned if anyone else shall. The critical faculty to you means a weapon by which you can spoil things for other people, people who would have been quite happy with them, and rightly, if you'd kept your mouth shut."

" Oh, I know," said Musgrave, following him closely, grinning the superior grin that meant his blood was up, " you'd have us all become as little children."

Johnny had got him to the other side of the stage now, step by step away from the tiny folded thing hidden in the arbour. Keep the argument going, and he was like a hooked fish. But how difficult it is to argue when your own mind is caught inextricably in another matter, a matter of life and death, which must at all costs be kept secret.

" Oh, no, I wouldn't say that," he objected, eyeing his opponent critically. " You must have been a horrid child, come to think of it, for ever sticking pins in other kids' balloons, and all for their own good. No, my dear chap, you stay as adult as you please, and wallow in your chilly intellectual experiences. But don't expect to enter the kingdom of heaven, either."

Off the stage now. Get him well away from it, ask him up to the office, if necessary, to look at the *Rosenkavalier* toys. " *Pastiche*," he'd call that marvellous, inspired heir to *Figaro*, without doubt, but let him. Anything, as long as his attention was never for a moment drawn to the arbour.

" I shall be staying through your performance of *Figaro* to-night," said Musgrave, pacing elbow to elbow with him along the corridor.

" By all means. Use my box, if you'd like to."

" Thanks all the same, but if it's all one to you, I'd like to hang around backstage."

He would! Johnny saw him for ever looming up, angrily smiling, between him and the small, damning thing that must be extracted and destroyed. There'd be no touching it again until to-night's performance was over; but some time, praise be, the man must go home and sleep.

Alone behind closed doors, Johnny sat down to think it out. Twice he reached out for the telephone to call Gisela, and once he even began to dial her number, only to drop the instrument in its cradle again without completing the call.

What, after all, could he tell her? And what could he ask her?

He knew now where the length of embroidered ribbon torn from Hero's baldric had vanished to, he knew where to lay his hand on it this minute, if only the watch-dog below could be called off for a quarter of an hour. Poppies, cornflowers and wheat embroidered on white silk and edged with gold thread, part of a ribbon from a Bohemian bridal head-dress, converted to serve as trappings for a child prince's dress sword, nearly two centuries ago. His fingers still burned with the touch of it, soft and fierce and clinging.

And no one but Gisela could have put it there.

That was a certainty. She had stood there concealed during Tonda's aria, and it seemed she had known already that she must get rid of this delicate, dangerous thing at once. She had to hide it there, where she was, before she went out to face the disaster that had fallen upon them all. It could easily be done without Nan's noticing, there in the dark.

Once done, the thing could not be undone; Musgrave's men were always about the place, there was nothing to be done but leave the thing where it was and show no interest in it, and hope that the enemy would go away. But the enemy had not gone away.

She had hidden it. She had known that she must hide it. She had known the reason for its importance, because she had known, she must have known, that Chatrier was already dead.

Whatever might be the truth about that night, Gisela had lied.

The final curtain came down on a *Figaro* as disappointing as it seemed to have been successful. Eight or nine curtain calls, a conservatory of flowers; but Johnny knew better, and so did all his team, even the brave and unlucky substitute Figaro who realised only too well that he was out of his class and struggling against the odds. The audience had the wrong feel about it; half of the seats, at least, were occupied by people who would not normally have gone near a Mozart opera, and had done so now only out of morbid curiosity, dropping in on the scene and setting of a sensational tragedy for kicks.

The same attitude would be reflected in the more popular notices, and the better ones would hold fastidiously aloof and be more critical than usual to avoid joining a fashionable stream. Unsatisfactory to everyone. Johnny was sorry for his Figaro. The boy had worked hard and done as well as it was in him to do, and it's bitter having to swallow the knowledge that your best isn't good enough.

He went out of his way to say a few words of appreciation and comfort to him at the end of it; not too effusively, because the boy was by no means a fool. I could make a fine artist of him, thought Johnny, if I could have him for a couple of seasons and find him the parts that are within his range. Why should he have to put up with being a bad Figaro when he has the makings of a pretty good Masetto?

The house was emptying rapidly, the receding hum of satisfied excitement, familiar but to-night curiously off-key, vibrated in Johnny's ears as he stood in the wings. The members of the orchestra were clattering out of their pit through the low doors, hoisting their instruments and drifting away to put on their coats and make for home. Their talk was of the iniquity of the licensing hours in these parts of London's outer fringe, and where you could get a drink notwithstanding, and the horse that fell down in the three-thirty, and Spurs' chances in the European Cup.

That was all right with Johnny; he knew all about the small realities as well as the great ones, and saw no quarrel between them. Some of Mozart's jokes were distinctly off-colour, and he had all, repeat all, the attributes of humanity. But the music—oh, the music!

The lady harpist, of course, was more genteel; she knitted in the intervals while the others played pontoon.

Johnny stood saying: "Good night! ... Good night! ... Good night!" to this one and that, and letting the evening disintegrate round him. He had seen no sign of Musgrave since the curtain fell. There had been three other plain-clothes men about the place, but none of them was in sight now.

Johnny set a course across the stage, in such a way that it would bring him close to the back of the left-hand arbour; and there under cover of the canvas he halted to light a cigarette. No one paid any particular attention to him, no one was close.

He knew already what he would find, but he slid his fingers between the wood and the canvas, and felt upwards to the spot where the folded ribbon had rested.

There was nothing there now. Only an infinitesimally

tiny fibre of white silk, three-quarters of an inch of thistledown, clung to the edge of the two-by-four where it had been.

She had had to wait a long time for her opportunity, but *Figaro* had provided it at last. The same hand that had hidden Hero's torn baldric had retrieved it again during the last act.

He made his way slowly and miserably to Gisela's dressing-room, knowing that he could not let it rest at that. He had never before hesitated to knock at her door; this time it cost him an effort. And even when she called him in, smiling over her shoulder from tired, dark eyes, he knew that he couldn't begin to ask her about it. After all the time they'd known each other, suddenly he found himself at a loss with her.

" Well? " said Gisela. " How did it go? "

She was still in Marcellina's black gown, with the stiffly boned bodice and the tiny waist. He came to her back, and stood looking down into the steady eyes that watched him from the mirror. She smiled, and he returned the smile; which of them had to make the greater effort was a question.

" As well as we could expect, I suppose. Pretty well, really. After what's happened we couldn't hope for an honest audience."

" It will pass," said Gisela, as though she could find no better comfort for him or for herself.

" I'm sorry, I thought you'd be dressed. I'll go away, shall I? "

He let his hand rest in the lace that made her milky shoulders whiter. She turned her head a little, her lips parted and her lashes low on her cheeks, as though for

a word or one more touch she would have laid her cheek
against his hand and rested so. He had never seen her
look so tired. There were tiny, fine lines at the corner
of her mouth, others like them round her eyes. His
heart melted in him with so sudden and sad a fondness
that he could hardly speak.

" Oh, girl, if only you'd told me! "

How often had he said that to her in the last few
days? And how often looked it, even when he was
silent?

" Oh, my dear, don't! How could I? By the time
I knew he was coming it was too late, we couldn't have
gone back on the contract. What would have been the
use of making you miserable, and starting all that again?
I thought we could make it work. I thought I could
carry it."

" But if I'd known! I'd never have let you." He
drew back hopelessly, sighing. " I'll go away," he said.
" You get dressed, and I'll take you home."

" No, don't go, you sit down here. I'll manage."

Her wardrobe had large double doors; she retired
behind their shelter, and he heard the long zipper of her
gown shirr softly downwards as she unfastened it.

" Hero was a little subdued to-night," said her
muffled voice from under the hooped petticoat as she
lifted it over her head.

" Aren't we all? " he said bitterly.

" She did very well. But a little muted, all the
same."

Her handbag lay on the dressing-table, close to his
hand. He had already known for some minutes what
he was going to do, but doing it was one of the hardest
things he'd ever undertaken. His body was between

her and his hands, so quiet there on the dressing-table close to the black calf bag. His broad shoulders would hide both the act and the image of the act in the mirror; from her, not from him. He would have to live with it, and with himself after it, as well as he could. And it might be all for nothing. A silly, obvious, frightening place to put something so dangerous, but women are queer about handbags, they regard them as sacrosanct by some special magic, even apart from any granted privacy.

" You're very quiet," said Gisela, installing Marcellina's dress on its padded hanger, and reaching for her own black jersey suit. " What's the matter? More than usual, I mean," she added wryly, for the weight of the shadow that burdened them all had become daily harder to bear.

" Nothing. Same complaint as Butch's, I suppose—just subdued."

His fingers eased open the clasp of the bag, very gingerly for fear of a sound she would be sure to recognise; but the rustle of the voluminous lace and taffeta skirts in the wardrobe covered his offence.

She was a tidy person, even her handbag was a model of order. Make-up, comb, purse, keys, handkerchief, cigarette case, lighter, two or three opened letters. Nothing more. Yes! In one of the letters, something soft and smooth that wasn't paper. He parted the folds, and there it was, the sudden bright, burning gaiety of gold and red and blue and white, putting out fine, wavering filaments to fasten on his skin like tentacles.

Between forefinger and middle finger he drew it out and unfolded it. Seven or eight inches of it, with a torn hem at one end, and strands of coloured threads trailing at the other; and obliquely crossing it, approximately midway, a straight, narrow line of dark, brownish-red, hardly thicker than a pen-stroke, and like a pen-stroke more strongly marked at its edges, where it frayed out a little, like an ink-stain.

A thin line of blood, incomprehensible but unmistakable, the blood of Marc Chatrier.

CHAPTER SIX

HE HEARD HER light step behind him, and felt the cold sweat break in the palms of his hands with shame and agitation. The ribbon was folded back into its envelope, the clasp of the bag closed, everything as she had left it, except for the stinging colour in Johnny's cheeks. The faint waft of *muguet* that shook out of her movements reached him and set him quivering. He had never been so acutely aware of her as now, when she couldn't confide in him, and he didn't know what to do to help her.

Her eyes met his in the mirror. He got up slowly, and turned to face her. For a long moment they were out of words. She hugged the collar of her fur coat to her pale cheeks, and picked up her bag.

"Johnny . . ." she said in a muted gasp.

He thought for one moment that she was going to pour it all out to him, but he should have known better; all she wanted was an hour off, time to regroup before the next engagement.

"Johnny, take me out somewhere. Anywhere, I don't care. Let's go and have supper at the Mezzodi Club, or something."

"If you like," he said, startled. "If you're not too tired."

"I'm not *tired*. I'm just wild to go somewhere else and do something else, and not see Inspector Musgrave's face while I'm doing it."

"I'll send Hero home with Tom," said Johnny

eagerly, " and we'll borrow her Aston and run into London."

" You don't mind?"

" Mind? I'll be glad. I need to get out of here, too."

And that was true enough, perhaps, but the answer to his problem wasn't going to be found in London any more than here, and how could he ever speak to her of what he knew? For years he'd relied on Gisela, worked side by side with her, thought aloud to her without a qualm, shown her the worst of him as well as the best, and trusted her to accept both and make do with him as he was. And she'd never attempted to restrain or change him, but neither had she ever withdrawn her loyalty and friendship from him.

He took her arm as they went along the corridor to Hero's room. The handbag nestled between their bodies, the symbol of her silence and solitude. She hadn't given him the trust he'd always given to her. And how could he wrest from her what she hadn't offered? There was no way round it. Nonplussed and miserable, he held her gingerly, afraid even the touch of his hand might betray how much he knew.

Where did he stand now? What was he to do? How was he to help her if she wouldn't ask for his help? And he felt her there against his side, so slender and so quiet, dearer than ever he'd imagined she could be, a revelation. She must be preserved, at all costs. Nothing was any good to him without her.

" We're going out to supper," said Johnny, putting his head in at Hero's door. " You don't mind going home with Tom, do you, Butch, and lending us the Aston Martin for to-night? Nella will have a drink waiting for you, and a sandwich. And sleep well, love.

You haven't got a rehearsal to-morrow, you stay in bed."

"Anybody'd think I was an invalid," said Hero affectionately, and bundled her coat into his hands for the pleasure, as she said, of being helped into it by her favourite male. How easy it had been to recover the old terms with Hero.

"It's just that you've looked a bit down, gal, the last few days." He wrapped his arms round her with the coat and hugged her warmly, her rumpled fair hair against his cheek. "Anything the matter?"

"Everybody in this theatre," said Hero resignedly, "seems to be going round asking everybody else if anything's the matter. Not really, darling. We had a murder on the premises, that's all. Funny, the way it upsets people. You'd never expect it." But she turned and hugged him in return. "Sorry! I'm all right, duck, don't you worry. You run off and spend all night dancing, or something. Do you both good."

They took her down with them. Her presence there between them on the way afforded them a kind of ease, because she put immediate confidences out of their reach, and enabled them to make believe fondly that but for her innocence they could have spoken freely.

In the foyer Sam was waiting for them, and as soon as they appeared he bellowed for Codger, who came running jealously to guard his privileges.

"He's outside," said Sam, in the tone which could only refer to Musgrave. "Been standing there ten minutes or more, swopping news with a couple of his buddies. Watch out he ain't got a cordon round the house when you get home."

"We're not going home, Sam. Butch here is, she

has to get her beauty sleep. But us young ones are going out on the tiles."

"Prodigal parent I've got," said Hero, gallantly playing up to him. She didn't even look round for Hans Selverer; he'd be gone long ago, and in any case, he'd shown pretty clearly, for all his half-hearted denials, what he thought of her, and on what terms he wanted to continue his association with her. Nobody, thought Hero sadly, is getting much out of this deal. "You come home tight and dent my car," she said warningly, "and see what you get."

Sam and Codger followed them out to the Bentley. It was early November, and moist and mournful, with a thin slime on the streets and a thin mist in the air, so that all the lights had faint grey aureoles round them. The decorative trees that fringed the semi-circular fore-court of the theatre had long since turned crimson, and there had been no frost as yet to bring down the leaves; but the sodium lighting and the moist air took from them all their colour and texture, and they hung shivering like faintly luminous grey rags on the branches, silent and sad.

In the apron of light the Bentley stood drawn up at the foot of the steps, with Tom Connard idling beside it, his great hands in his pockets, his enormous jut of bony brow ape-like over the kindest and most knowing eyes in the world. The cigarette that clung to his lower lip was whipped smartly out and trodden into the thin mud as soon as he saw his skipper approaching. The details of their relationship were laid down by Tom, not Johnny; Johnny had never been a stickler for the hierarchies even in the Navy, and not much of a respecter of ranks and persons himself, for that matter.

There were still a few other cars about the forecourt, just warming up and switching on their sidelights to drive out to the road. And there was Musgrave's black Austin, pulled right round into a strategic position close to the exit end of the sweep of tarmac, where he could make a quick, smooth and unobtrusive departure at whatever moment he pleased. Even the lights tailed out there into dimness, and the glisten from every moist surface of road and coachwork and kerb and masonry tended to blend the car deep into its background.

Midway between the Bentley and his own car, Musgrave himself stood on the bottom step talking to two of his men. As though on an expected signal, he broke off his colloquy as Johnny reached the pavement, and walked away towards his Austin at a brisk but casual pace.

Johnny's thumbs pricked. The way the car was positioned might be the fruit of experience and instinct, the lingering until he came and the departure when he came might mean nothing but that Musgrave wanted to assure himself that events were pursuing their normal course this night as on other nights. But added together they suggested a more exact and deliberate concern with his movements than he liked to contemplate. For himself he didn't care, it could hardly matter less how much sleep Musgrave lost over him; but the little, folded thing in Gisela's bag turned his heart sick when he thought of it.

" You've only got me to-night, Tom," said Hero. " We're swopping cars for once, Johnny's going on the town."

" Very good, miss," said Connard, generously giving way so that Codger could open the door for her.

" No, the front, Codger, love, I'm going to ride with Tom. That's fine! " She turned back for a moment to offer Johnny a chilly cheek. " Good night, darling! Good night, Gisela! "

" Hey, how about your keys? " said Johnny.

" In the car. I garaged it, so I didn't bother to bring them out."

Codger slammed the door firmly upon her, pulled to make doubly sure his work was good, and stood back, beaming. The Bentley pulled away. Round to the left the black Austin had its lights on and its engine running and was heeling round very, very gently towards the road. It let the Bentley go by, halt at the exit, and turn majestically into the open road. It had seemed that the Austin was about to follow, but it did not. Its exhaust continued to breathe faint blue fumes for a moment, its engine to purr experimentally, then it was drawn more closely into the side again, and the hum of the motor ceased. In a moment the driver's door opened.

So that was it. And now they knew where they stood; but at least Hero was off home out of it. He didn't want her, he wasn't interested in her. As soon as he saw that she was alone in the car apart from the driver, he abandoned the Bentley. He was waiting for other game.

" The bastard! " said Sam softly between his teeth, watching him start back towards them. The two plain-clothes men had turned and mounted the steps into the theatre to keep the watchman company. It wouldn't be difficult to find something that ought to be said, in ordinary courtesy to the owner of the place.

Johnny thought of Gisela and himself shut into the car shoulder to shoulder, as close as lovers and as far apart as the poles, unable to communicate, unable even to face this danger as one creature, as they had always faced everything from their first flight together in the dark. Always they had had that unity. Even the broken, shocked creature he had snatched out of the ambushed transport had instinctively fastened in him the last remaining root of her faith in man, from which the whole marvellous plant had sprung again. Now they had nothing. He, who had always taken it for granted that he would be the first person she'd come to for help, was powerless now to help her.

Suddenly such a desolation of rage seized him that he shook from head to foot, and the approaching figure of Musgrave quivered before his eyes like a broken reflection in a pool.

" Blast him! " he said through his teeth, in a muted howl of frustration and despair. " I wish somebody'd do me the favour of knocking *him* off! "

For that one instant he meant it; it was like a convulsion of pain jerking through him, turning his blood to gall. Then it was ebbing, and he shook with the feebleness and shame it left behind. He licked his lips, and the bitter taste of sweat was there, and his forehead was dewed with cold.

" You don't have to worry, son," said Sam at his shoulder, only just above his breath. " There's nothing he can do. You hear, Johnny? " A hard old fist rapped at his ribs behind, knocking home the text. " You'll be all right," said Sam.

" Famous last words," said Johnny, with a grin that hurt him, but looked all right.

The weakness and nausea ebbed away after the mutilating rage; he took hold of the affair as it was, and stopped thinking of what it should have been, because Musgrave was very close now, and there was no time left. He didn't think anything was due to happen here; he thought Musgrave was more interested in letting them go their own way for the moment, and waiting for things to happen of themselves, provided always that he was there to see. But because of the ribbon in Gisela's handbag the danger was acute. She couldn't be left alone with Musgrave now, not even for the time it took to fetch the car round from the garage.

" Sam," he said, in a voice now quite calm, " would you mind giving Norrie a ring and asking him to bring Butch's car round? And don't you bother to come out again, it's chilly out here."

Luckily Musgrave probably hadn't learned enough about the Leander Theatre yet to realise how out of character it was for Johnny to ask to have his transport brought round for him at all when Tom Connard wasn't there; ordinarily he'd have been round the corner himself after it, like a terrier after a rat. But those were the aspects of things that Musgrave didn't pick up so quickly.

" We'll be all right," agreed Johnny softly, and returned Sam his nudge in the ribs to start him up the steps.

He looked round then for Codger, but Codger had already disappeared. He'd be back; no good telling *him* not to bother, shutting Johnny safely in the car was one of the main moments of his day, and he wouldn't care which car it was, either.

" I think I ought to tell you," said Musgrave, blandly arriving, " that I'm leaving a man here overnight. You've no objections? "

" No, I've no objections," said Johnny. " Would it be indiscreet of me to ask whether you're expecting something to happen? "

" Not expecting. But no harm in hoping. And he can put in his time studying stage furnishings, without the complications of rehearsals and performance going on all round him."

" He has my permission to poke wherever he fancies. I hope he likes his tea strong? That's the way he'll get it if he hasn't brought his own. Or there might be stout, if he's lucky, Martin isn't a beer man. What is this, a last fling? "

" We never give up," said Musgrave, with a not unpleasant smile. " I know you gave me a blanket permission to go ahead at the beginning, but I thought I'd just mention it." He drew back a step, his eyes slipping smoothly from face to face. " Good night then, Mr. Truscott! Good night, Miss Salberg! " And yet another step. He was turning on his heel as he said: " A very creditable performance to-night."

" The patronising bastard! " said Johnny under his breath, a faint but controlled gust of the old fury shaking him. He had it in better focus now, he knew that by rights it did not belong to Musgrave. But the ache within him would not be eased. She stood silent in his arm, so pale and mute and calm that he could not bear it. If only she'd let him in!

The Aston Martin came sliding sweetly round into the arc of tarmac, and Norrie, who looked after all the cars and lived over the garage, hopped out of it grinning with pleasure, and held open the door for them. Poor old Codger was missing his treat; in his own way he'd complain of it for days, and everyone would have to

devise new excitements for him in compensation.
Johnny expected him to come darting down the steps
anxiously at the last moment, but he must have been
somewhere out of sight and earshot, safe with Sam, for
he did not appear.

Musgrave was just climbing leisurely into his Austin
as the sports car slithered by and halted at the exit. Very
nice timing, hardly a pretence at all, only a cloak of
decency for the benefit of both hunted and hunter. Not
a disguise, merely clothing. It argued at least a kind
of respect for his opponent.

Johnny swung the car left, towards London. Traffic
was light, and the moist night curiously silent. They
might have been a thousand miles from the city, and yet
all the unpeopled trappings of town life were strung
along the way, eerie and pale, livid in the ghostly lights
on either side of them. A few walkers on the footpaths,
but so few that they, too, were muted and distant, like
ghosts.

" Speak, girl! " said Johnny, his eyes on the mirror.
" How will I know I've got a woman with me, if she
won't talk? "

The Austin had rounded the curve into the road
after him, and was following sedately on his tail, not
bothering to lie close.

" He's following us," said Gisela, small and still
against his shoulder.

" I know. Don't worry, I can leave him standing
once we're in the decontrolled stretches."

He was driving very demurely, because he had to
think as well as drive, and because he wanted her, with
all his heart, to take this opportunity of confiding in
him. There was nothing he wouldn't do for her, if only

she'd let him, but she was still mute, she asked for nothing.

What was he to do if she still shut him out? What *was* he to do about this woman of whom he found he was so damned fond?

If she wouldn't talk, that made his thinking all the more urgent. She had lied, and she was hiding evidence. Not evidence that would in itself convict anyone of murder, but extremely suggestive evidence, none the less; and more damning than the thing itself was the act of hiding it, and the persistence and length of her silence about it. The ribbon had been torn from the baldric of the sword used to kill Chatrier, and it had Chatrier's blood on it.

And it had been found where only she could have hidden it.

So the provenance of the thing alone made it legitimate to begin to reason from the premise: *If* she killed her husband . . .

He went on from there; the Austin all the while following him at a civil distance.

If she killed her husband, then it *cannot* have been after she entered the arbour, for from that point on she was with Nan Morgan until after Tonda fell over the body and screamed. That is absolute, whatever objections there may be to it.

Therefore Figaro was dead *before she entered the arbour*.

But he sang his two asides afterwards. No, *he* didn't, because he couldn't have done, he was dead, that's given. Correct the former statement: *Somebody* sang his two asides after she entered the arbour. There was no doubt at all that Figaro had sung his aria himself, for he had had the stage to himself and been in full view of hundreds of people until the end of it, when he retired into the trees. Only those two lines from hiding could have been sung by someone else. Could they? By another baritone, even a good mimic, as so many singers are? Yes, in this case they could. Angry, sardonic asides, hissed in a half-tone, with hardly more personality than a whisper. Yes, another baritone could have done it.

Hans Selverer.

Too clearly, too positively, Johnny saw the whole course of that evening. A joint revenge. Gisela had picked up the rapier as she had said, but she had not disposed of it as she had said, she had quite simply brought it down into the wings in her voluminous skirts, walked into the darkened pine-grove and used the sword on Chatrier, and then calmly gone on-stage; and Hans, with two short lines, had given her an alibi afterwards. Hardly more than five minutes in all had been gained by that act, but it had been enough to place her well clear of suspicion. Perhaps an instantaneous conspiracy, all achieved in those few minutes, perhaps an impulsive act on the spur of the moment, undertaken by Hans of his own volition.

There remained a number of unanswered questions. Why did she take the baldric away with her afterwards? There was blood on it, yes, but all the same, why didn't she just drop it with the scabbard, beside the body? There was nothing in the thing itself to connect it with her more than anyone else. If she'd left it there, what would it have told the police more than they knew already? Bloodstain and all?

" He's closing up on us," said Gisela, her chin on her

shoulder, her eyes narrowed against the following head-lights. The street lighting was thinner here, they had left the shops and cinemas behind, and were threading row upon row of suburban dwellings, with elaborate pubs on every crossroads; but still in such a ghostly quietness. The country has no such solitudes as the less frequented urban spaces at night.

" I know," said Johnny bitterly. " And I'm doing forty. He's a cop, he can afford to shove it up above the legal figure, but he needn't think he's going to get me picked up for speeding."

He couldn't read anything in Gisela's voice; she merely made the remark as though she had gathered from his manner that he might be interested, as though the whole thing had nothing to do with her.

And what resolution and self-control she had shown throughout, simply hiding the ribbon in the best place available to her, and then for a whole fortnight never casting even so much as a glance in its direction, never making the fatal mistake of trying to recover it until the next performance of *Figaro* ensured that she could do so in privacy. And now to have it actually on her person the very night when Musgrave chose to keep her under observation!

If I weren't here, thought Johnny, she could quite simply wind the window down and throw the thing out, once we pull away from Musgrave over the heath. By the time it's lain in the gutter overnight and had a few wheels or feet over it, nobody's even going to stop to look at the colours, much less pick it up. The roadmen would sweep it up with the rubbish, and nobody any the wiser. But she can't do it, because Musgrave isn't the only one who mustn't know. *I* mustn't know. And

I can't tell her that I know already, not only because I'm ashamed of spying on her, but even more because having trespassed once doesn't give me any right to trespass again. And he thought again, my God, what am I going to do if he decides to take a chance and pick her up to-night, before she has an opportunity to get rid of it?

The derestriction sign waved its bar dexter at him. The lights, strung thinly here like gold beads on a chain, made scattered islands of radiance in a thicker haze between the trees of the open heath. The houses fell away, and left them in a startling urban solitude.

The Austin was close now, but lying decorously back from the Aston's tail. Johnny's foot went down smoothly, and the little car leaped forward like a hound let off the leash.

He was drawing steadily away when he saw in his wing mirror an abrupt and unaccountable convulsion seize the Austin's lights. They lurched sideways towards the verge, recovered for an instant, and then suddenly plunged wildly across the road at speed, out of control.

Gisela turned in the passenger seat, her fingers cold on his arm, her eyes flaring.

"Johnny, what's happening? He *can't* . . ."

Tyres screamed ineffectively, sliding on the moist road. The crash shivered the night's quiet into fragments. A broken beam of light bowed into the bottom of the hedge; the second eye was blinded. Another crash, dull and echoless, like metal crushing under an enormous foot, followed the first. By then Johnny had braked fiercely, and had his door open and was out of it and running back along the road almost before he had cut the engine. Shuddering, the quietness came back, settling like a startled bird reassured. Only Johnny's running footsteps troubled its placidity. The Austin was still enough now.

Gisela clawed her way out of the car and ran after Johnny, her handbag clutched under her arm; even in emergencies women cling to their handbags.

She saw Johnny come close to the crumple of metal that was the Austin, and baulk at what he saw. He heard her coming behind him, and turned to catch her in his arm.

" Go back! Please! This isn't for you."

" Yes," she said, panting, " I'm all right, I can help. What *happened* to him? "

" God knows! "

He put her behind him, he had no time to argue with her. He turned to the shattered car. It had hit the lamp standard head-on, and wrapped its broken face about the metal base until the bent shaft was nearly hidden in the crumpled sheets of black paintwork and chrome. The left headlight dangled loose from the wreckage, spilling wiring, like a gouged-out eye. The upper part of the standard had snapped clean off and dropped across the roof of the car, crushing it. The front passenger seat was collapsed like a tin can in a press; but when Johnny darted round to the right-hand side he saw that the driver's door lolled open and undamaged, scraping the ground, and a huddled figure prostrate on the road was just dragging his feet after him from the interior of the car.

He hoisted himself up groggily from the slimy tarmac, and got his feet under him, stunned eyes wide open but blind, just in time to mouth a throatful of incoherent sounds and collapse into Johnny's arms. But he had stood, he was alive, death had discarded him.

Johnny took the weight neatly, dropping to put a shoulder under Musgrave's hips. He hoisted him carefully to the grass under the trees at the roadside, propping his head with the scarf he stripped from round his own neck. Musgrave was breathing, hoarsely but regularly, and Johnny could find no obvious signs of injury.

" My God, but some folks are lucky! If that door hadn't burst open . . ."

Musgrave's glasses had flown off when he was flung out of the open door; they lay broken in the gutter, their splintered lenses refracting gleams of faint, sourceless light.

Behind Johnny's back Gisela said, " Johnny . . ."

Her voice was low and muted; it took him a moment to realise why it made his hair rise in the nape of his neck. That hushed sickness of horror brought his face round to her wary and still.

" Johnny, there's somebody else in the car."

There couldn't be. It was absurd. Musgrave had clambered into his car alone, and certainly stopped nowhere on the way. Yet Johnny laid the unconscious man's head hurriedly back on the folded scarf, and came to his feet in frantic haste.

" In the back seat. Somebody——"

She was half in at the hanging door, kneeling in the frost of broken glass that whitened the driving seat, squeezing her shoulders against the unbelievably crumpled junk of metal that sagged into the rear of the car. A hand and an arm lolled over the back of the driving seat. She was feeling her way with shivering, tentative fingers up the sleeve towards a shoulder trapped and flattened cruelly under the weight of the standard and the roof as it was driven in. Shallow and hard, moaning breaths gushed out of the tangle of wreckage from a face close to hers. There was blood on her hand.

Johnny took her round the waist and drew her back, and she turned suddenly with a cry of understanding and love and pity, and wound her arms about him.

" Johnny, it's *Codger*! "

He didn't say anything, he just froze in her arms, for one instant absolutely stiff and still; then he had put her aside and was in the car, thrusting, heaving, tearing hands and wrists on jagged edges as he fought to lift away the weight that held the crushed body prisoned. His hand touched a feebly moving jaw, stroked its way up a cheek sticky with blood.

" Codger, old lad, I'm here, Johnny's here. Hold on, boy, I'll get you out. It's me, Codger . . . it's Johnny . . ."

A faint sound, between moan and speech, answered him out of the tangle, and something in the very tone of it told him he was known. Whether his voice had penetrated the darkened and lonely mind, or whether his very presence spoke its own language to some inner sense, Codger was aware of him. Johnny worked his left hand painfully under Codger's armpit, gripping hard in the stuff of his coat.

" Gisela——"

" Yes," she said, quivering at his shoulder.

" See if the rear door will open." He rested while she tried, keeping his hold, spreading his back against the sagging roof.

"It's buckled." She had a foot braced against the running-board, her weight thrown back, pulling with both hands.

"I know——but I think the catch has burst, it might give. Careful, don't hurt yourself."

The top of the door gaped, started out of place. With a hideous grating of metal the lower part gave to her pull, and the door was open. She leaned into the car, stretching an arm to support Codger about the body. Her sleeve tore against jagged edges of metal, but she gripped and held.

"Good girl! If I can shift this an inch or two, try to ease him clear."

Crouching, he got a foot on the seat, and thrust upward with braced shoulders, panting, setting his teeth. He had felt the slight lurch above him of a weight settling afresh; it was not so much a matter of lifting it as of disturbing it. The lamp standard had crashed on the left side of the car and crushed it. Johnny's contortions shook the lopsided shell, and the weight slid farther to the left. The buckled metal, relieved of the oppression from above, lifted slightly with the force of its own tensions, and Johnny felt it give, and heaved with all his force.

Codger slid backwards out of the vice, and Johnny, scrambling after, helped to lower him with aching care and anxiety into Gisela's arms.

"Let me take him."

He came round to lean into the car behind her, and she let his arm replace her own, and edged past him to stand clear, waiting until she could lift Codger's trailing legs and help to carry him to the grass.

Johnny held the distorted, crushed body in his arms,

stooping over it a forehead running with sweat as he wiped blood away from the battered face.

The large, blank eyes opened wide, staring unfocused into the night. A convulsion of doubt and loneliness and fear quaked through him. A core of solitary terror, deep within and tenacious to the end, beat frantically about its prison for company and comfort.

" I'm here," said Johnny, close to his ear. " I've got you, it's all right." Nobody had ever heard Johnny's voice sound like that, except Hero, perhaps, when she was three years old, and he had suddenly to be two parents instead of one.

Codger's mouth moved, fought for a moment with the old constrictions, and then forgot them utterly. A thread of a voice, heart-rendingly apologetic for failure, said faintly but coherently: " Sorry, Johnny! I done it all wrong—botched it . . . Sorry! "

" You did fine," protested Johnny staunchly, not even understanding then what he meant, not even realising that his poor mute had expressed himself plainly at last; and he kept on saying it, steadily and soothingly, until it penetrated his senses that Codger had stopped listening.

CHAPTER SEVEN

JOHNNY LAID HIS BURDEN back in the grass, and got stiffly to his feet.

"I'm going to take the car and go back to the first house there, and call the police. See what you can do for Musgrave." He took a couple of steps, and looked back for an instant. "You don't mind being left?"

"I don't mind," she said.

Almost inevitably some car or other would be along and stop at the scene any moment; the marvel was that they had had the night to themselves so long, though it had been no more than ten minutes in all, he found, when he thought to look at his watch. Better wipe his face and hands, and not burst in on some suburban housewife looking like a murderer fresh from his crime. He used a handkerchief as best he could on his scratched cheek and stained palms, and whirled the car round in the width of the road. There was a house only a hundred yards or so back, the last of its kind for half a mile, and certain to be on the telephone. Better call the ambulance, too, while he was about it. It wouldn't be any use to Codger, but Musgrave might need it.

He drove like an automaton, and said and did what was needful. He felt nothing yet, only a stunned coldness that was probably shock. He didn't think, he didn't reason, the functions of his own personal mind had stopped; social man, civic man, did what was required of him.

When he got back to them Musgrave was sitting up

in Gisela's arm under the hedge, and there was a dark Morris drawn in close to the wreck. The newcomer had provided brandy, apparently, for Gisela had a flask in her hand. Better still, the kind donor was by no means anxious to linger if he could be of no further help; no doubt he had a wife at home waiting for him, and by the look of him probably a family, too. If the police and the ambulance were already summoned, and there was nothing more he could do, he thought he'd better be on his way.

Johnny thought so, too. He wasn't anxious to have any unofficial observers present during what was to come.

" Then I'll leave you my card, in case I should be needed."

He was still addressing himself to Johnny, but with a respectful eye on Musgrave, too, an accurate measure of the inspector's rapid and dogged recovery.

" Thanks," said Johnny, " but I don't suppose they'll have to bother you. We'll stick it out. We have to, anyhow, but that's enough."

" Terrible thing," said the relieved Samaritan, gratefully withdrawing. " So sorry about your wife—dreadful for her. Wonderfully brave! "

He drove away uncorrected. Maybe there really was something about them that made them look married, or maybe it was the done thing to assume that two respectable-looking middle-aged people driving about together late at night should have the benefit of the doubt.

The words stayed in Johnny's bludgeoned mind when the speaker was gone, like a spark in bracken, smouldering unseen in the roots of his thoughts. My wife. A long time since he'd even run the phrase over his tongue. It had a bitter-sweet taste, stimulating and evocative.

He took a rug out of the car, retrieved Gisela's coat, and gently covered Codger's body. It seemed already to have contracted, to be strangely low and at home in the grass, as though it were already returning to earth. Johnny closed the large, puzzled, patient eyelids over the fixed eyes, and turned abruptly to those who were still alive.

"Here, girl, better put this on. I'm sorry we've managed to ruin it for you." He turned her about like a child, and fastened the single great button under her chin. "Sit in the car, love, and try not to feel too much of anything. As soon as I can I'll take you home."

He wasn't too surprised when she didn't do it. Women had always liked Johnny, but they'd never obeyed him; and that was odd, considering how little trouble men had ever given him in that way. She was close beside him as he lunged forward quickly to lend Musgrave an arm to lean on, for the inspector was climbing unsteadily to his feet.

"Now, take it easy, man, your fellows will be here soon. I've called them, and the ambulance, too, and you'd better stay a patient for to-night, I should think."

"I'm all right," said Musgrave obstinately. "This is my case, as long as I'm on my feet. I'm quite capable of carrying on now. You got him out, didn't you? Miss Salberg told me. Where is he?"

He kept hold of Johnny's arm to hold himself upright, for the world swung when he turned his head; but the dry authority had come back into his voice as soon as he was master of his senses.

Johnny nodded silently towards the place where the car rug was spread over Codger's body. He still found it hard to grasp that that was all, that one of his friends, dependants, children, was gone; troublesome, no doubt, in his way, but does that make you feel any differently towards your children?

Musgrave went down on his knees gingerly, and turned back the rug. The dead face ignored him, already sunken into its own inscrutable fantasy, where he had no rôle at all, either as friend or enemy.

" He tried to kill me," said Musgrave quietly, his voice suddenly fully alert and aware. " Or did you know that already? "

" *He did what?* " said Johnny faintly, hearing his own words echo to him out of an infinite distance, and unconscious even of Gisela's hand closing warmly on his arm.

" Tried to kill me." Musgrave repeated it no less quietly, looking up at him over the silent body. " You didn't know, then? What *did* you imagine he was doing here? "

" *Codger?* " He clutched his head, holding his disintegrating mind together. " He was the gentlest soul who ever breathed, he wouldn't hurt a fly."

" Oh, yes, I think he would—if he thought you were being threatened, Mr. Truscott. You, or anyone belonging to you. Was he the gentlest soul who ever breathed when he graduated through that special training course of yours during the war? And what do you think *this* was for? "

He had pushed back the rug from the right arm, and lifted the large hand that curled indifferently at Codger's side. He drew up the cuff and showed a thin cord dangling from the clenched brown fingers. Not long, no more than eighteen inches, tethered to a waisted toggle at either end. Black cord, close-textured, probably waxed.

" And how do you think I got *this*? "

Musgrave pulled down the collar of his shirt and strained his chin upward, to show a thin groove scored across the right side of his neck, strung here and there with beads of blood.

" And this? "

He held out his left hand before Johnny's eyes, and a similar groove marked its back, and broke the skin below the base of the little finger.

" He was in the back of the car. Quiet as a cat. All I saw was a change in the degree of light in the mirror, suddenly, as though something had cast a shadow. I didn't hear a thing. I don't know why I put up my hand, but that's the only reason I'm alive now. Just a reaction against a feeling of movement behind me. The cord went round hand and all, and he couldn't tighten it. I half blacked out, and lost control. But I'm alive."

Death had kicked open the driver's door and ejected him. The dog it was that died.

" Ever seen a thing like that before? "

Musgrave laid down the hand in the grass, and clambered weakly to his feet again. Johnny was standing staring down at the trailing cord with dilated eyes, his face motionless and numb.

Yes, he had seen similar cords many times. Just one of the many ways of killing silently. Men who were to survive and continue useful in Johnny's wartime trade had had to know as many of them as possible; no man can master them all. Codger's unco-ordinated mind had never excised those skills, his hands had never forgotten them. There'd been no spastic tremor when he flicked the cord round Musgrave's throat and drew it tight; only the blind instinct of fear and the upflung hand had saved him.

Johnny stiffened knees that threatened to buckle under him, and suddenly the fingers closed tightly upon his arm seemed to be all that held him upright, or kept him from covering his face and howling his anguish to the night.

He knew now what it was Codger had botched. " I done it all wrong. . . . Sorry, Johnny! Sorry! " Only now did he understand what he had heard.

" Oh, my God! " he said helplessly. " My God, my God! "

The hum of cars coming rapidly, not yet shut between the trees; the distant alarm of an ambulance bell at the last crossroads.

" That won't be needed," said Musgrave, and went down on his knees again to feel his way through the dead man's pockets, without any great hope of revelations; what could such as Codger Bayliss be carrying about with him? The garrotte was an atavism, a mechanical memory, violence re-enacted in innocence; there wouldn't be two such prodigies.

" I don't know or care," said Johnny, in a voice that creaked with effort, " whether you'll take my word for this, but for my own peace I want to say it. I didn't send him. I had no idea what he meant to do."

" He knows," said Gisela in a whisper.

Musgrave looked up, his bruised eyes flashing from

her face to Johnny's. "Strange as it may seem," he said, "I don't doubt you. I can imagine you doing murder, Truscott, but not getting somebody else to do it for you. Not even a man in his right wits. If it came to it, I'm pretty sure you'd do your own killing."

"Thank you. I suppose I should be grateful for that. And yet you understand, don't you, that he wasn't to blame, that he couldn't be held responsible for what he did. I took on the responsibility for him, and this is how I've carried it."

I done it all wrong—botched it. . . . Sorry, Codger! Sorry!

"Your conscience doesn't come within my province," said Musgrave dryly. "You must sort that out yourself."

"Blast you, I wasn't offering it to you, or asking your advice about it, either. I'm telling you we've somehow managed to kill off an innocent between us, no matter what you choose to call him."

"I'm concerned only with facts. Facts like a length of cord round my neck, Mr. Truscott. Or . . ."

His hand came out of Codger's left-hand jacket pocket holding something that looked at first like a rolled-up handkerchief. It uncoiled on his hand like a living thing, bursting into a glow of colours under the headlights as a sleepy fire bursts suddenly into flames.

"Or this," said Musgrave, his voice sharp and quivering with eagerness, vented in a great sigh of achievement; and he stretched out in his two hands before Johnny's eyes eight inches of embroidered silk ribbon bright with poppies and cornflowers and ripe

golden wheat, the torn end of Hero's baldric, slashed
with Marc Chatrier's blood.

"I'll go, then," said Johnny, halting just inside the
door. "If you're sure you'll be all right?"

"You won't come in? I think you need a drink,
Johnny."

"Not now. We'd better get some sleep."

It was nearly three o'clock. The world seemed to
have completed an entire revolution in those three
hours of the night.

She watched his face with hollow dark eyes, hazed
with weariness, and felt him withdrawing from her
moment by moment into a private place where he kept
his deepest griefs, and where, it seemed, even after all
these years she was not allowed to enter.

"Johnny, are you all right?" Ridiculous phrase,
but one used it for every degree of well-being from the
merest subsistence to bliss; and he would understand.

"I'm all right," he said.

"Do you know you never said one word all the way
home?"

"What was there to say?" he said drearily. "He's
dead. He tried to kill Musgrave, and Musgrave is
about to prove that he killed Chatrier. And I made a
fine mess of taking care of him, if I couldn't keep him
from getting involved in this job. But it's too late to
say anything. It's done."

"I wish you could have been spared this," she said
in an aching whisper, meaning the bereavement and
self-reproach and the pure pain of Codger's death.

"I wish I could," said Johnny, meaning the knowledge he would have given his right hand not to

possess, but of which he could never now be rid. He
hadn't said a word, he'd let the thing happen as she'd
willed it, because he wasn't supposed to know, and
what good could it do Codger now to turn and betray
Gisela? Hadn't he been thrashing his mind for a way
in which she could get rid of the baldric safely, without
even admitting him to the secret, since it seemed she'd
die before she'd do that? Well, she'd found a way.

Still half-dazed, Musgrave had never questioned his
discovery. Why should he? He'd opened his eyes to
find two people bending over him, and one of them an
innocent stranger, whose very presence was a guarantee
of the correctness of Gisela's behaviour. Why should
he inquire exactly when the convenient witness had
arrived on the scene, and whether Gisela had been
there alone for some minutes before his coming? He
had one murderer, why be in too big a hurry to look
for another?

Maybe in her place, thought Johnny, I should have
done the same. There was Codger dead and safely out
of it, and Musgrave unconscious, and no one else by,
and it was now or never. Codger couldn't be hurt any
more. Maybe I should have planted the thing on him,
too. How can I tell? Who am I to blame her? Was
it so terrible to leave him to carry both loads, when he'd
already incurred one? Who am I to judge her? Who
am I, for God's sake, to judge anybody, the mess I've
made of my responsibilities?

Let it go, then. He felt that Musgrave was satisfied,
that he would never be able to resist this neat, well-
rounded ending. Somehow every detail would be fitted
into the pattern of Codger's jealous and protective
passion. It would be interesting to see the pieces of the

puzzle ingeniously tailored into place. Why look for a second criminal, where one so obligingly offered himself?

" Then—if you won't come in——"

" No, I'd better get home. In the morning I shall have to tell Hero."

He saw Gisela flinch, and suddenly, as though a curtain had been drawn from between them, he saw every least imprint and mark of her history in her face, the set of her lips, indrawn and pale, the tight white lines that marked her slender bones in jaw and cheek and brow, as though they were fretting their way through the skin, and above all the silent, uncomplaining endurance of her eyes.

In all the time he had known her he had never seen tears in them, but he knew the look they had when there should have been tears, and her reticence and courtesy insisted on containing them.

" Good night, then, Johnny."

" Oh, girl, girl! " he said in a great sigh of pity and resignation and bewilderment, and reached and drew her to him, folding his arms round her and holding her to his heart. Her cheek was cold against his. He kissed her very gently, and turned and went away without saying another word, suddenly so tired that when the door was safely closed between them he could hardly fumble his way down the stairs.

" So the case," said Musgrave, " can be regarded as closed. You must have been expecting that, I suppose. With one would-be murderer already known, it hardly seemed very probable that there should be another one hanging around in the same comparatively restricted

group of people. It could happen, once in a while, but
the odds are all against it. But this—this turning up
in his pocket more or less clinched it."

He spread out the strip of silk on Johnny's desk,
leaning over it with a thoughtful frown, and with something of human satisfaction, too, in the set of his
features. New glasses with a more fashionable winged
shape had given him an oddly quizzical expression, and
made him look younger. The thin line on his neck, like
a faint brown pencil-mark, was fading rapidly. His
brush with death had left, as far as could be detected,
no other mark on his nature or his mind, not even a
touch of awe and humility.

Johnny sat looking down at the beautiful, radiant bit
of brightness, the gold-thread ears of wheat, the scarlet
and blue of the flowers.

" A normal man would have burned it long ago,"
said Musgrave, kindly explaining to him the workings
of the minds of all men but himself. " He had plenty
of opportunity. I suppose he kept it because it was so
pretty, and gave him pleasure to handle and look at."

" I suppose that could have been it," said Johnny
woodenly.

" So he carried it around with him, a fortnight and
more after the murder. Curious that after all the
hunting we'd done for the thing, it should be put into
our hands so simply at the end of it."

" Extraordinary," said Johnny, without joy or
wonder.

He put out a hand, and moved one fingertip gently
back and forth above the torn end of the baldric, and
the fine, waving filaments of silk rose and clung to his
finger. Magical stuff, silk. You could smooth it on to

the wall, and it would cling there, too. Or perhaps the weight of the embroidery would be too much for it and bring it down. He touched the ruled line of dull brown that was all that remained of Marc Chatrier's blood.

"You're wondering about that," said Musgrave with a slight smile.

"In a way, yes. Such a curious sort of mark. No doubt it tells a detailed story to you, but I haven't been able to make much of it."

"Well, I suppose these are small professional mysteries. You have others as complex in your own field."

"But I leave you yours," said Johnny, with the first faint gleam of humour and malice. "You're sure you're not making too much of this? Does it really make a complete case in itself? It looks a bit flimsy, lying there alone."

"Possession of it was almost more revealing than even what the ribbon itself can tell us. The thing has been missing ever since the night of the murder, it was clearly torn away in the course of the murder; and after that it turns up again for the first time in Bayliss's pocket. Who but the murderer was likely to have torn it loose and removed it? I admit I didn't pay enough attention to Codger Bayliss in the first place. He seemed to me too simple and harmless to conceive such an act, let alone carry it out. These cases can be very complex. Who knows what goes on inside their minds?"

"Who, indeed?"

The thought of Codger, imprisoned within his speechless world and struggling to communicate with the world outside, made Johnny's heart turn in him

with a convulsion of sickness. And yet had Codger been
more isolated than the rest of human kind? If he could
not reach a hand to Gisela, nor she to him?

"And that stain . . . that *is* blood, I suppose?"

"It is, and the same group as Chatrier's. There can
be very little doubt that it *is* Chatrier's. Which takes
us a step further. And then, the form of this is
peculiarly interesting. And so were some of the details
of the wound, though I didn't tell you that earlier. It
seems that the point of deepest penetration showed
signs of a double thrust, as though an attempt had been
made to withdraw the blade, and then, finding it too
difficult and having no time to make a job of it, the
murderer had thrust it back in and abandoned it. At
the farthest point of the wound, for no more than a
minute fraction of an inch, this dual penetration showed.

"Now, what we think happened is something like
this. Bayliss was upstairs with Mrs. Glazier in the bar
all through the third act and for part of the fourth, then
he slipped away unnoticed, and he was down in the
wings when the alarm was given. No one was clear
about exactly when he arrived there, but with so many
people moving about that isn't surprising, and they
were all quite used to him. It seems probable that in his
own way he had been disturbed for some days by the
unrest he felt around him, and by a feeling that
Chatrier was making himself a nuisance and perhaps
even a danger to you. He's in the wings when Chatrier
sings Figaro's last-act aria and withdraws into the pine-
grove to hide. Chatrier's back would be to Bayliss, his
eyes naturally on what was going on on the stage.
Bayliss has found Miss Truscott's sword where Miss
Salberg put it ready to her head. It's a pretty thing in

itself, and the broken baldric is even more attractive.
He's playing with it when Chatrier backs towards him.
I've seen he was used to ways of silent killing, and
you've confirmed that he had training in those
techniques. Was he also, in his time, expert with knives
and bayonets?"

"He'd handled every kind of steel. But it's a long
time ago."

"He hadn't forgotten what to do with a cord, had
he? So he has a very fine, keen sword in his hand, and
your enemy backing on to it . . . and he follows his
instinct, and kills."

"So efficiently? Not a murmur out of Figaro?"

"I didn't tell you this, either, but Figaro's lips were,
as you might expect, marked by slight but unmistakable bruises. A hand was clamped over his mouth.
And the sword, I think, was gripped through the
baldric, which is why there were no fingerprints on it
but yours, Selverer's and Miss Truscott's. Figaro falls,
and dies probably within a minute. Bayliss knows
enough to lower him gently to the boards. He then
tries to pull out the sword, but it's lodged fast, and he
hardly succeeds in moving it. But in that attempt,
which he very soon abandoned, I think this mark was
made.

"He can't shift it by pulling from the hilt, he tears
off this end of the baldric, which is already dangling
loose, and through it grips the blade with his right
hand, close to the body, and so tries to ease it out. He
moves it a little, and in doing so encourages the very
slight bleeding. I don't know if you've noticed, or if
you remember off-hand, but the sword has some very
fine chasing up the edges of the blade near the point,

and the blood had been drawn *up* these grooves for a few inches. Here he held the blade through this ribbon, and the edge over which the silk was folded left this stain on it. You can see what a thin, straight line it is."

"I had noticed. It was puzzling me. You make everything very plain. And the other edge didn't mark it, or cut it?"

"Try holding a very sharp blade through a fold of silk. You don't shut your hand on it, you fold the silk round the edge that's towards your palm, and hold the centre of the blade firmly between fingertips and thumb. The rest of the ribbon hung free. The threads weren't cut because there was no actual pressure against the edge, and no friction. But these very fine roving strands took up the blood and retained this stain. And then he gave up, because it was inevitable the alarm must be given any moment. He left the sword and scabbard, but he took his piece of ribbon away with him—perhaps at first hardly realising he was still holding it, but afterwards he kept it because he liked it, and it seemed no harm."

"I see. Everything explained," said Johnny, with a hollow smile.

"It leaves nothing unaccounted for, I think."

"Nothing. I congratulate you."

Musgrave folded the strip of silk again carefully, and slipped it back into the plastic folder in which he had brought it.

"I know you were fond of the fellow, Mr. Truscott. I know it's a tragic case. But be thankful it's over. You can go ahead with your work, now, with an easy mind."

" May I tell my people the case is closed? To some extent the cloud's been over us all."

" Yes, of course, tell them. They have a right to know." He rose, buckling the straps of his briefcase. " Miss Truscott's sword can be returned to you very soon. And the inquest—yes, an ordeal, I know, in the circumstances, but it'll soon be over."

" I don't think Hero wants the sword back," said Johnny, going to the door with his visitor. " She's upset enough about Codger, I don't want her to see it again. But there's one thing I did want to ask you . . ."

Musgrave halted in the doorway, looking back with an encouraging smile. " Yes? "

" After the inquest—I don't know the drill when a case ends like this, without a trial. Shall I be able to claim his body? I'd like to take care of the funeral."

" Yes," said Musgrave, after a long moment of studying him in silence, " I think I can promise you that you shall have his body."

The word had gone round within the hour.

A shadow lifted from the Leander Theatre and its company as the news passed from lip to lip. Johnny told Franz, and Franz told the morning rehearsal of The Magic Flute. Inga, a truly electrifying Astrofiammante, spoke to Tonda, her Pamina, for the first time in ten days voluntarily and even civilly. Max Forrester, an imposing Sarastro even in slacks and a sweater, remarked to Monostatos that celebrations would be in order, and Monostatos agreed that the Blackcock's Feather, just round the corner, would be open any minute.

In the regions backstage the shadow that had fallen some days ago kept the sky still cloudy, and Codger's place in the corner of Sam Priddy's box ached with emptiness. But even there some urgency of heart began to lift from them, and left them looking forward instead of back.

But the news fell with the most profound effect of all upon Hans Selverer.

Papageno turned with a face suddenly full of shining purpose, put down his magic chime of bells with a ringing peal, and walked unnoticed out of the rehearsal. When next they should have heard his voice there was blank silence, and the birdcatcher was nowhere to be found. Such a thing had never been known to happen before; he was normally a very conscientious young man.

Hans was looking for Hero. He knew she had come to the theatre with her father that morning, though he had not seen her since. She was not anywhere about the stage, she was not in Johnny's office, she was not in her own dressing-room. Hans knew at least where to ask after her next.

He put his head in at Sam's box, and there she was. She was sitting lonely in the most retired corner, where Codger Bayliss had so often sat with his knitting, and it seemed she had inherited the function with the seat, for she had Codger's unfinished sweater on its plastic needles before her, and was counting stitches with a deep frown of concentration. She went on counting even when Hans came in. The narrowings at the top of a sleeve can be tricky when you have no pattern, and are following in the steps of somebody who has left you no clues.

"Hero!" said Hans, and halted, unsure of his English though not of himself.

She looked up quickly, grey eyes flaring wide. For two days they'd lost their clarity and brightness, crying in private over Codger; but she was nineteen, and her world was full enough of people to repair the hole torn in it by the passing of one among so many. The sadness that lingered in her face was the impending shadow of maturity. She looked at him in doubt and astonishment, and with something of offence, too. He had been avoiding her for days, and now he walked in on her with a bright, possessive face, as if he owned her.

"Hero, have you heard that this case of Figaro is now closed? But officially. Franz has just told us, and he had it from your father."

He sat down beside her, and looked grave for her sake, but still he could not help shining.

"I know you are sad, and I am sorry about Codger, you know I am. But now I am able to come to you and ask you something, a thing I could not ask before." He took the knitting firmly out of her hands, careful not to spill the stitches, and laid it down at a safe distance; and because the spark of indignation was alight suddenly in her eyes and her colour was rising, he made haste to take possession of the hands he had thus emptied, in case she should slip out of his reach and run away from him.

"I wish to ask you if you will marry me," said Hans firmly, looking her in the eyes with those gentian blue eyes of his that had been so steadily staring in the opposite direction for the past week and more.

The kindling flush left her cheeks abruptly, her lips fell apart in a gasp of astonishment, wariness and, of all

things, consternation. She had imagined such a
moment fondly in her own private fantasies times out
of number, and while there had seemed no possibility
of its ever being translated into reality it had seemed
to her the last prodigy of human bliss. She had even
imagined her own response to it; but never like this.
Now that it was suddenly pitched into her lap in good
earnest she reacted to it with a strong impulse of panic
and recoil.

It was too soon, too sudden, she wasn't ready. She
was only nineteen, and it wasn't something you could
undo in a year or so if you didn't like it—not the way
the Truscotts understood it, anyhow. And she hadn't
been anywhere yet, or seen anything, or sung half the
rôles she wanted to sing. And then, just *one* man, and
you couldn't whistle up another one when you got
bored, or sort your dates by the half-dozen and shut
your eyes and draw for it. Even if you did want him
very much, even if you were sure you loved him very
much, it took a bit of thinking about to jettison everything else for him. And the end of it was unreasoning
rage, for he shouldn't have sprung it on her like this,
without any warning or any time to think.

" No! " she said, not manœuvring any longer, but
in plain and resolute retreat. She tried to withdraw her
hands, but it wasn't so easy. He was taken aback, but
he held on; perhaps he couldn't believe his ears, or
perhaps he simply didn't intend to give up so easily.

" Hero, you must know that I am in love with you.
These things women always know."

Someone must have told him that, perhaps one of
the older women who found him so irresistible. Inga,
maybe.

" You have a nerve, Hans Selverer! " she said hotly.
" All this time you've been avoiding me as if I had the
plague, you could hardly say ' Good morning ' to me.
And now you come making up to me, and expect—
expect——"

" Not *you* had the plague, Hero, but *I*. Don't you
see how hopeless was my position until this case was
solved? That Inspector Musgrave, he believed that *I*
had done it. He knew about my father, and he thought
—he was sure—I had killed this man. How could I
ask you to have anything to do with me? How could
I try to make you like me better, when I was suspect
like that? "

" I don't believe you care anything about me," she
persisted, holding her reeling defences together against
the assault of his near presence, with treason already
budding in her soul. " It isn't much of a way of
showing you love a person, to refuse her a share in your
worries. *Anybody* can be generous with the good
things."

" If I was wrong I am sorry. I could only do what
I thought was right. But now I am free to tell you how
much I love you, and to ask you——"

" But you don't, you can't! You called me a spoiled,
self-willed child."

She turned her head away from him, straining out
of reach, aware of the crumbling walls of her resistance,
and fascinated by the spectacle they made as they
toppled. The very crash might be rather glorious.

He loosed her hands and took her by the shoulders,
drawing her to him. He was smiling, not too confidently, but with some childlike trust in her ultimate
will to acceptance, as though he knew her better than

she knew herself, but didn't want to flaunt his knowledge too openly.

And after all, she was beginning to think, resigning herself to the next world like a drowning woman, there might be compensations. Just one man might not be a bad thing at all, provided he was the nicest, the most gifted, the most attractive man around, and the one every other girl coveted. And there was also the consideration that when a man like that did ask you, you couldn't afford to take any chances on whether he'd feel like asking you a second time.

" *You* called *me* a priggish busybody. And it was not true, I was only very alarmed for you, and very jealous."

" You mean it *was* true what you said about me. You said Johnny ought to beat me——"

His arm slid round her shoulders. She flattened her palms against his chest, but they seemed to have no force, and in a moment her right hand stole up the lapel of his coat and round his neck, and settled there with fingers spread in his hair and the taut lines of his nape fitting snugly into the palm. He was at once warm and cool to the touch, and sent tremors of delight to her heart.

" I didn't mean it," he said against her cheek, " I was only angry. And you know, in opera it is always the wife who beats the husband—like Susanna and Figaro. So marry me . . ."

" No! "

He kissed her so nimbly that it was possible to pretend she had never uttered that negative, and he had never heard it. And then he was moved by a stroke of inspiration to invite himself into the family by a formula she could not resist.

" ' *Pace, pace, mio dolce tesoro!* ' " pleaded Hans very softly in her ear.

She heaved a deep, helpless, happy sigh, and: " Yes yes! " she said, and tightened both arms round his neck.

The walls fell, and the crash was glorious.

Hans went up the stairs with a firm tread, a bold face, a smudge of lipstick just in front of his left ear, and no doubts at all of his reception until he reached the door of Johnny's office. After all, he was a person who had something to offer, a rising reputation, ambition, a sufficient income, tastes triumphantly in common with Hero's, and a character which was now threatened by no shadow. All the same, the inevitable constriction gripped his middle as he rapped at the door and answered Johnny's somewhat restrained: " Come in! "

" Mr. Truscott," said Hans, looking at his prospective father-in-law across the desk with a face of such earnestness that Johnny's mouth fell open almost before the shot was fired, " I have the honour to ask you if I may pay my addresses to your daughter."

Now I wonder, thought Johnny, charmed in spite of his astonishment, what wonderful phrase-book he got that out of!

" Well, well! " he said, swallowing down the shock with difficulty. " This comes a bit suddenly, a man needs time to think about it. And ultimately, let's face it, fathers don't have much say in the matter these days. You sit down and keep quiet while I get my breath back."

Hans declined the chair he was too restless to stay

in, and demonstrated his nervousness by going on talking.

"I love your daughter very much, but you will understand I could not address her while I felt myself to be under suspicion." Luckily he had no way of knowing how that ran into the quick of Johnny's senses. "And it matters to me very much that we should have your approval."

Johnny got up from his chair, to be free of the blue, disconcerting eyes, and walked to the window to stare down into the forecourt littered with dull, dead leaves.

"And Hero," he said without turning his head, "how does she feel about it?"

That was pure stalling, because he had to have time to think. He'd seen the little pink bow that decorated the boy's ear, and the ravages that hadn't quite been combed out of his thick brown hair. Give him that, he'd hardly been able to get up the stairs fast enough for Father's blessing. And it made sense of things he hadn't understood, things that had complicated all their lives. Not that he ever would understand his daughter. Or women in general, for that matter.

"She has done me the honour to accept me. If we have your permission, of course."

"Hero never said *that*," said Johnny positively, and a brief, lop-sided grin shook his face out of its anxiety for a moment. "Oh, I know, I know! She's a good kid, she wants me to be happy about it, too. But look, I need time to think. I've got to get used to the idea. I've hardly realised yet that I've got a grown-up girl, and here I am threatened with losing her. She's only just nineteen, and if she's going to get herself set up for life I need to be sure she's getting it right."

" Naturally," said Hans, " that I perfectly understand. If you wish us to wait, to make sure—*I* am sure, but I will wait for her as long as you think right."

" Yes, well . . . Suppose you leave me to think it over now. Don't worry, I won't keep you waiting long, but I'd like to be left alone to-day to come to terms with the thought. Take her out somewhere until this evening, take her home after the performance. Take care of her, and come and talk to me to-morrow."

He felt acutely the confusion of mind in which he was sending Hans away. He'd expected, perhaps, a pretty thorough grilling, but an inevitable welcome into the family in the end. Why shouldn't he? He knew his worth. There was something wrong here, some reservation he didn't understand. And yet to be told to take the girl out for the day argued that her father had a certain amount of confidence in him.

" As you please," said Hans stiffly, discouragement damping his voice; and he went away with somewhat subdued dignity. What he would tell Hero Johnny couldn't guess. Maybe it would bring her hot-foot up the stairs to confront her awkward parent and demand to know why he hadn't flung his arms round her suitor's neck at once, as apparently she had. But no, she wouldn't do that. In deference to her new lord she'd be all duty and loyalty, and leave him to conduct his own business. She might even feel for the old man, thought Johnny wryly, and want to make the upheaval as little of a shock to him as possible. She was a nice kid, even if she was a handful. Maybe he ought to have asked Hans if he knew what he was tackling.

And now he was alone the problem lay there before him in all its crudity and ugliness, and not all the contortions he might essay in the effort to put himself in other people's places could make it look any better to him. He couldn't very well feel happy about entrusting his girl to a young man who had been an accomplice in a murder, and who apparently didn't in the least mind letting a poor old imbecile take the blame.

A fine singer, a potentially great artist, a pleasant and good-natured young man, he was all that. It wasn't that Johnny had any holier-than-thou thoughts about him, it wasn't that he didn't like him; he did like him, very much. But giving him Hero was another matter.

So now there was no help for it. He would have to talk to Gisela.

CHAPTER EIGHT

THE COUNTESS STEPPED out of the right-hand arbour, alone, erect, regal even in Susanna's pert soubrette clothes, her voice clear and still as it severed the clamour of recriminations and pleadings and rejections seething round her disguised maid. Frozen, they stared at her, even their exclamations hushed to awed undertones; and Susanna slowly uncovered her face, the deception happily over and the battle won.

The Count, who had sung like a man possessed all the evening, cajoling and menacing and lording it as never before, excelled himself now in his moment of utter defeat; and suddenly it was clear how right Mozart had been to give him only those last four words to say for himself, without bluster or anger or defence of any kind, simply:

" ' *Contessa, perdono,*
perdono, perdono! ' "

Clear, too, why the answer came so simply, the lovely, rounded, melting phrase of forgiveness. When she told him: " I can't say you nay," she was telling the final, absolute truth not only about the end of this adventure but about their turbulent married life. No one could have resisted this Count. He could have led any woman a dog's life with his caprices and his jealousy, and still wound her round his finger at the end of it when he gave in and admitted his enormities thus

167

engagingly. Even though she would know, as doubt-
less his Countess knew, that the whole thing would
happen all over again within a month.

Inga extorted her tribute of dimmed eyes and
absolute silence, melting and wringing all hearts. The
whole group echoed the same caressing phrases. And
then the end of the finale, fresh and gay and harking
back strongly for the wind of happiness, ready to
dance all night.

The curtain came down on forgiveness, reconciliation,
hope.

Johnny left his box and went round into the wings
as they came off-stage after their flurry of curtain calls.
The fine, satisfying sound of an audience going away
happy soothed his ears; he knew that full, fed note of
content very well, now, he was sensitive to every
variation in it.

Cherubino, seeing him there, made a brief, impetuous
detour into his arms, hugged him breathlessly, and was
hugged again almost too exuberantly.

" Hey, my *ribs!* Were we good to-night? "

She knew the answer, she was glowing with achievement.

" It was *him!* He got us all on the run. Even Inga's
forgotten she was standing on her dignity. She *con-
gratulated* us! Imagine that! "

" Oh, so he's taking it for granted he's got you, is
he? " said Johnny, nettled. " Bragging about his luck
already! "

" No, *he* isn't. *I* told them. It's all right, isn't it?
I didn't exactly tell them, actually, it just sort of started
busting out all over me, and I had to explain."

She had no doubts at all, no qualms about his re-

actions. How could anyone resist her Hans? She
locked her arms about Johnny's neck, and hugged him
again warmly.

"Darling, I'm so happy! It's all right if I go and
have a little supper with him, isn't it? I'll be right
home afterwards."

"Since when," said Johnny, "do you ask my permission before you have supper with a bloke?"

She blushed at the reminder, but without any dim-
ming of her state of bliss. "Since right now. Not that
I'm afraid of you, just make a note of that. I love you,
that's all."

"Well, come to that, I'm pretty soft on you."

He turned her about in his hands. "Go on, then,
get off with you, you baggage, and be good." He
started her off with a pat in the fluted skirts of her blue
coat, and she took to her heels and ran like Cherubino
himself for her dressing-room and her own clothes.
The rapier that danced at her hip now was a mere
property sword; nobody would ever commit murder
with that.

So it seemed the whole company must know by now
that Hero considered herself engaged to Hans Selverer.
Time and events were hemming Johnny in, even her
innocence and confidence conspired to force his hand.
There was no help for it, he must go to Gisela and have
it out with her to-night.

"Good night!" he said to the members of the
orchestra on his way along the corridor, and: "Good
night!" to Nan, slipping out blushingly in the arm of
the youngest 'cellist. "Good night!" to Don Basilio
and Doctor Bartolo, hurtling out as one man, head-
down for the stage-door, en route for the Blackcock's

Feather round the corner; they had practically five minutes left before closing-time. "Good night!" to Tonda, tripping down the stairs in her mink, her arms full of flowers and her eyes full of self-satisfaction, energy and mischief. Business as usual in the Leander Theatre, it seemed, and everything back to normal, even tempers. The hole Codger had left behind him would soon heal, except for the few who had had large tracts of their own lives and whole aspects of their own personalities torn out with him.

Johnny climbed the stairs with a tired step, and knocked at Gisela's door.

She was sitting before the mirror in her old candle-wick robe, taking off Marcellina's make-up. Mezzo-sopranos are perpetually condemned to sing mothers and duennas and housekeepers. He had once had a great scheme for presenting her as Carmen, but she had firmly put her foot on that. She hadn't the voice for it, she said, and she hadn't the temperament. And she'd been right, as usual, he'd had to admit it in the end. Annina, the intriguer, with the foreign accent and the itching palm, would be a pleasant change from middle-aged frumps when they staged their new *Rosenkavalier* next season.

He closed the door behind him, and stood for a moment leaning against it, watching as she loosed her long hair out of the elaborate dressing and began to brush it. He knew she had seen him come in, their eyes had met for a moment in the mirror. Words did not come so easily now, the effort that preceded speech made the very air in the room seem tight and rarefied, too thin to keep alive. They still drove home together as before, always hopeful that the old ease would return, always straining with small, hesitant acts of consideration and tenderness to conjure it back again. They could not draw together again, and they could not separate; separation was unthinkable. Apart, they would die.

" Good audience to-night," he said, coming to her shoulder.

Her eyes lifted to his face quickly, sensing something more than usually askew about the mirror image.

" What's the matter? "

When she questioned him directly, like that, her voice intent with partisan affection and anxiety, the impalpable barrier between them shuddered and almost cracked, but never quite.

" Nothing," he said. " Merely a little problem in responsibility. Young Hans came to see me this morning, after Musgrave had gone, after I'd told Franz to let the company know it was all over."

" Ah! " said Gisela with a pale, bright smile.

" Yes . . . you've heard, of course. Everyone seems to know already. It seems he's been nursing a notion that he was still suspect number one, and now that he finds he isn't he's come right out and told me he wants to marry Hero."

Her face had kindled into affection and pleasure, and even a brief, flashing glimmer that might have been laughter, until she saw the shadow that hung on his lowered eyelids.

" You see, that was how the wind was blowing, after all. When they took to being so polite to each other I thought I'd been mistaken. To-day she's been shining so, no one could miss it."

The silence when she stopped speaking was marked. She laid down her hairbrush, watching him with eyes suddenly wide in wonder and anxiety. " You're not glad. She's in love with him, Johnny. This isn't just play. They're in earnest."

" Apparently," said Johnny. He had picked up the silver ribbon that had bound her hair, and was twining it round his fingers. " She'd left her brand on him plain enough." His voice was as cloudy as his face. She watched him, alert and still, the dark curtain of her hair half-veiling her eyes.

" I know, Johnny. It is very early. She is very young. But it was bound to happen. Just look at her! And he's surely a very suitable match for her, and a very good young man. You won't be losing her," she said, touching very delicately where she supposed his pain was.

" No, I know. Not losing a daughter, but gaining a son. I know! Though I admit it does come as a jolt to know it's on me so soon. They grow up too fast, you can't keep pace with them."

" What have you said to him? "

" I haven't given him an answer, not yet. I told him to come and talk to me to-morrow."

" But Hero seemed to be sure——"

" But I'm not," he said, with a sudden flare of trouble and anger. He put down the ribbon, and came round to the side of the mirror to have her face to face. She saw how compulsively he closed his hand upon the edge of her dressing-table; the large, long bones stood white in the brown of his fingers.

" Marriage is no joke, Gisela, marriage is for life, and don't forget this is my responsibility. She isn't of age. I can at least hold things up for nearly two years if I think it necessary—long enough to give her time to think better of it. Not that I don't like him. I do. But——"

He had arrived at it by ill-judged and unhappy ways, but he had arrived. It came out not angrily or cruelly, but with a helpless and inflexible simplicity.

"What am I to do? *You* tell me! He was your cover, wasn't he? He sang the two lines that put you out of the running, safe in the arbour with Nan. And Codger being written off as the killer doesn't seem to worry him, he's as happy as a sandboy now he's in the clear. Not that I can blame either of you for hating the fellow," admitted Johnny, "and not that I've any right to judge. Still . . . A man prefers his son-in-law not to be an accessory in a murder. But what am I to say to Hero if I turn the boy down?"

Gisela had heard him out in stillness and silence, the sudden blaze of understanding in her eyes burning down into a steady glow. Her hands lay in her lap stiff and motionless. It seemed to him that for a moment she held her breath.

"I know where the lost piece of Hero's baldric was hidden," said Johnny, "because I found it there. And I know nobody but you could have put it there, and nobody but you could have taken it away again. You or Nan, and why should Nan do any such thing? But I made sure," he continued doggedly. "I looked in your bag, while you were changing that night. So I knew it was you who put it in Codger's pocket afterwards. And if *you* had killed Chatrier, then it happened earlier than we thought, before you went into the arbour. So there had to be somebody who sang

Figaro's asides for him after he was dead. And that was Hans—wasn't it?"

Her lips moved, saying soundlessly: "Yes."

"So what am I to do? Liking him is one thing, but giving him my girl is something very different. It isn't that I'm so spotless a lamb, God knows! But this is Hero's future, not mine. If you know the answer, you tell me."

She sat staring at him for a long moment still, her eyes wide and deep and stunned, and then the calm of acceptance came upon her, and the whiteness of strain began to fade out of her face. She got up quietly and went to the wardrobe, and lifted out of it Marcellina's rustling black dress. She brought it to him in her arms. "Look," she said, and unzipped the slender, boned bodice.

Marcellina was a compound of anachronisms. Not only did a zipper close her laced gown, but the busks that stiffened the bodice were slightly flattened spirals of wire covered with smooth plastic, instead of whalebone. A whole cage of springy supports ran from neck to hip, and the two front ones, one on either side of the zipper, were slightly larger than the others, and slightly stiffer. The seams were not sealed at the neck, but only closed by the fold of the lace-trimmed hem, so that the busks could be withdrawn at will. Gisela turned back the fold from the left-hand one, and drew out the top of the plastic-coated spiral a few inches. It was more rigid than would have been expected, and in a moment Johnny saw why. She turned the open end downwards and shook it, and with finger and thumb coaxed out of it something long and bright, with a small round knob at the end. As soon as she had the knob clear of its sheath the rest came out easily, and she held it up in her hand for him to see.

A strong steel knitting-needle, the old-fashioned kind nobody uses in these days of improving plastics. About nine inches long, but in its knitting days it had been longer; and filed down to a long, needle-sharp point that turned it into an efficient and deadly dagger.

He took it from her and looked at it closely. A faint film of a stain dulled the point end for several inches, though there was nothing material there under his fingers, only the discoloration. He looked up at her over the incomprehensible thing, and she saw that his hands were trembling.

" Sorry! " said Johnny. " I'm dumb, you'll still have to tell me."

"Did you not see that he had some new blue needles for his eternal knitting? Hero has been trying to finish his work for him—go and look at it, if you wish. And then remember how many years he had *these*."

The trembling had reached his body. He moistened his lips with a tongue almost as dry, and said in a creaking whisper: " Are you really trying to tell me that *this*——? *Not* the sword? But the sword was in him."

" Yes, the sword was in him. But the sword didn't kill him."

" Girl, do you know what you're saying? Are you sure? "

He took her by the arms and held her before him, shivering suddenly, shaking her with his bewilderment and exhaustion and grief, and the tiny flame of hope and ease at the heart of all. " How can you be so sure? "

" I'm sure," she said, " because I saw him killed. In front of my eyes, almost within touch of me. And I'm sure about the needle being the thing that killed him, not the sword, because, God help me, I know he was dead when I pulled out the needle, and drove the sword into him in its place."

Deep within the turmoil of his mind a small core of quiet came into being, as there had been, so it seemed, a core of justice, however lame and inadequate, at the heart of the tangle of Marc Chatrier's death. He took the foaming bundle of Marcellina's skirts out of her arms, drew her with him to the ottoman by the wall, and made her sit down there. He went on his knees beside her, and held her fast by the hands. He did not yet realise for the chaos she had made of his ideas that the barrier and the distance between them had been wiped out. He could touch her, he could hold her hands, he could question her and answer her questions.

Codger's mutilated knitting-needle lay beside her on the green brocade. A dual penetration in the last fraction of an inch of the wound, Musgrave had said—signs that the sword had been slightly disturbed in an attempt to withdraw it, and then thrust back again. Musgrave could fit everything into his theory. It seemed it was perfectly possible to pick the right man and get everything else wrong.

" You didn't really think," she said, her hands clinging suddenly to his with a desperation that belied the composure of her face, " that I could make a good job of sticking a rapier into a man's back? Silently—while he was *alive*? "

" Girl, how could I know what you had it in you to

do? You or any other woman? Or any man? I don't know much of anything, and what I do know I get all wrong. You tell me. You should have told me then, right from the start."

"How could I? Above all, I wanted you not to know. I couldn't feel that he—that the guilt . . . And you loved him!"

"And don't I love you?"

He shut both her hands gently in one of his, and with the other stroked back the long hair from her forehead and cheek. He didn't even know what he had said, it had slipped from his tongue so naturally.

"So that was why you took the needle away and hid it, because knitting-needles would have led straight to Codger. I know! I can imagine!"

For years they'd all been sharing the responsibility for Codger. How could she let him go bewildered and frightened into custody, and then to trial, however kind the law might prove, however surely he would be found unfit to plead? How could she, being the person she was, let him be taken away and shut up in an asylum? She must have acted so quickly, so instinctively, that thought had hardly been involved at all.

"I told you the truth about picking up the sword and bringing it down with me," she said, "but not about the reason. I never thought of killing anyone. I did try talking to him, I did threaten him, even, to make him leave you alone. I said I could make trouble for him if he made trouble for you, and so I would have done. What would it have looked like for him if I'd told some Sunday newspaper the whole story of our marriage, and what he did to me? But that was all, because I was sure it would be enough. He had as much to lose as you, maybe more, and he wasn't a fool. And then I tripped over Hero's rapier in the passage outside her door, and I saw the baldric was broken. So I brought it down with me. I didn't stop to ask any questions about how it got there, because I thought at first that if we were very quick we could put a few stitches in it to hold it for the rest of the evening, and give it back to Hero, but then I saw there wouldn't be time. And that's why I had it in my hands when I came into the wings."

It was all entirely in character. She was the tidier-up, the mender and tranquilliser and smoother of ends about the place. It was always Gisela who took care of the little things.

" I was early for my entrance. And you know how dark we had the stage, and how complex the set is. Tonda and Inga were somewhere to my right, but nowhere near me, Max and Ralph were over on the other side. And *he* was on the stage singing his aria, and then he backed into the pine-grove, almost towards me. There was someone standing there under cover, waiting for him. I didn't see or hear him until he moved a little to keep directly behind Figaro. And I didn't understand, I never realised . . . we were all so used to seeing him about the stage, he went where he pleased. There was no reason why I should even wonder. And then—he simply slipped his left hand over Figaro's mouth, and the needle into his back, there in front of my eyes, before I could move or speak. It didn't seem possible it could be done so smoothly. He just lowered him in his arm and let him lie, and he never made a movement again."

Her voice had grown thin and fine with wonder and

terror, not of death so much as of its silence and
suddenness. Even killing a chicken, even hooking a
fish, had more struggle and conflict about it than this.
He held fast to her hands, and thought of the act
almost as an achievement; for that was the spirit in
which Codger had learned the art of silent killing. He
made no mistakes about the things he did know. He
had forgotten the names of his brothers and half the
events of his own life, but he never forgot his acquired
skills, and his hands could still reproduce them.

" He was dead," she said, " before I even touched
him. He'd left him there—just lowered him to the
boards and slipped away and left him. And I . . . the
knitting-needle was so childish, so obvious. I thought
of him on trial, and of you . . . Or perhaps not thought,
I doubt if I did think. It simply happened to me. I
pulled out the needle. There was almost no blood. It
wasn't even difficult. I tore the loose end off the baldric,
in case, and held it with that, but there was nothing, not
so much as when you cut your finger. I wiped the
needle on the piece of silk—so that had to vanish,
too . . ."

As simple as that, the curious diagonal line over
which Musgrave had exercised so much ingenuity.
Nothing to do with the chasing on the blade, just the
thin mark left where she wiped the needle.

" And then I unsheathed the rapier, and put the
point to the wound at the same angle, and . . ."

A sudden convulsive shudder ran through her, but
her face remained fixed in a stunned and wondering
calm, and her hands, starting and quivering for an
instant like frightened wild things in his, sank again
into a warmer ease.

"The wound would have given away almost as much as the weapon, I *had* to mangle and disguise it somehow. You can do anything if you have to. I don't remember much about it now," she said, staring back wide-eyed into the memories she had disturbed, "except that I did it."

Just as well, thought Johnny, seeing before his eyes the thin, tell-tale stroke of blood on the bright silk, and the slender blade swaying upright, its point in Chatrier's back.

"And how did Hans get into it?" he prompted gently. Keep her talking, make her pour out the whole of it, empty the darkness and share the last of it with him, so that there should never again be so much as a shadow between them. He knew now that he couldn't bear another such banishment.

"He didn't do anything, he didn't know anything, there wasn't any conspiracy. He simply came into the wings ready for his entrance, and he must have seen me get up from the body and run on-stage. I was nearly late on my cue. I didn't know he was there until I turned to go into the arbour, and then I looked quickly to see if the body showed at all, and there he was. Standing right beside it, staring at me. I knew by his face he'd seen me, I knew what he was thinking. Such horror, and such pity! I couldn't guess what he would do. I couldn't do anything about it, whatever he did. So I just went on into the arbour. Then I was all right, then I had time to think, time to hide the ribbon where you found it, and slip the needle into the busk of my dress."

"And Hans gave you what he thought you needed, an alibi."

The boy must have made up his mind in about twenty seconds, for Figaro's first indignant comment came only three lines after Marcellina's retreat into the arbour. Johnny heard again vividly with his inward ear the final bitter: " ' *Il fresco—il fresco!* ' " Maybe Hans had had qualms about his act afterwards, maybe he'd deeply regretted it, but he'd stood to it stoutly even when he feared he was himself beginning to figure as chief suspect. No, there was nothing there that need make a man hesitate to confide his daughter's future to Hans Selverer. On the contrary, such stubborn loyalty was not easily to be found, and Johnny knew how to value it.

" He never had time to think, either," she said, " only to feel sorry for me."

" Does he know now? That it—wasn't you? That you only intervened to protect Codger? "

" Yes, he knows now."

" And when the alarm was given and the police took over, of course, you had to leave the ribbon where it was, and let it take its chance. And the needle, too? Do you mean to tell me that thing's been in your dress ever since? Even when the dressing-rooms were searched? "

" They were searched for the first time while I was still wearing it. And then, they were looking for the baldric, not for a knitting-needle. I knew there was a certain risk in leaving it where it was, but it seemed to me much more risky to try and move it while the police were always here among us. I knew I could get the ribbon back as soon as we gave *Figaro* again, and the best way not to draw attention to it until then was not even to look towards it or think about it. It wasn't so

surprising that they didn't find it, you see, because it
was perhaps the one place where they took it for granted
it couldn't be . . . Nan and I being in there together,
by their reckoning, from before the murder was committed until after it was discovered. When I did
recover it I meant to get it away out of the theatre and
burn it. But you know what happened."

Yes, he knew. After all her patience and courage
and resolution, after the days and nights of going about
her business with a composed face and keeping her
own counsel, all to save Codger, Codger had undone
all her work with his own hands.

" When you left me alone with them, that night, I
didn't know what to do. Codger was dead then. He
couldn't be saved, and you couldn't be spared. It was
too late to do anything but pick up what few pieces I
could, and it seemed to me the best thing I could do
was hand Musgrave his evidence, let him make his case
as it stood. There was no way of getting Codger out
of the blame this time, and he couldn't be hurt now.
So I put the baldric in his pocket for Musgrave to find.
Maybe it was the wrong thing, I don't know. I was
frightened of the complications I'd made, now that they
were no more use I only wanted to be rid of them."

" Girl, girl! " said Johnny, drawing her into his arm
with a groan of self-reproach. " What you've gone
through alone! "

" It wasn't quite so bad then. Not even quite so
lonely. After that night I told Hans . . . to put his
mind at rest. And it did something for my mind, too.
He's a good boy, Johnny, he'll never let her down, you
can be sure of that."

" But why didn't you tell *me* the truth then? You

could have, then. It was over for Codger, there was no need to hide it any longer."

"If I'd known you knew the half of it, like him, of course I'd have told you the rest. But I didn't know, you never said anything. Why didn't you tell me you knew I had the baldric? Then I should have told you everything."

Why didn't you tell me? They were both asking it; they could lose so soon the sense of helplessness and isolation, shake off so soon the state of separation where speech was a burden and confiding an impossibility, however much goodwill, however much love they brought to the struggle.

"And then, I didn't want to involve you in anything I'd done. I thought you were better out of it. One of us was enough to be tangled in all that. Poor Codger!" she said, and turned and rested her smooth forehead for a moment against Johnny's cheek.

"Poor Codger! But better that way than the other. If they'd taken him away from us he'd have died of fright and loneliness. But that you should have to go through all that for him!"

"It was mostly for you," said Gisela with the shadow of a smile warming the drained pallor of her face.

"Well, don't you ever do anything like that for me again, that's all. It scares the living daylights out of me when I think I've lost touch with you. We'll dispose of this thing now. You and I, together. We can, now. Musgrave's gone, and the case is closed."

And not, it seemed, so unjustly as he had thought. There was a kind of providence in it, after all. And she was back with him, he saw her clearly, his voice could reach her, they were saved. Never risk that again, never in life. He knew now that he couldn't manage without Gisela.

She drew herself gently out of his arm and rose, drawing breath deeply as though she had cast off a burden as great as the one she had lifted from him. " I must dress. No, you sit there, don't move. And you won't have to turn Hans down, after all, you see. All he did was take pity on me."

" I'm glad," said Johnny. " He's a fine boy, and they'll make a grand team. If he can manage her."

" He'll manage her. She'll see to that."

It sounded like a recipe for a pretty good marriage. Johnny, thinking of his darling, began almost to look forward to the excitement and promise of her dazzling career beside Hans Selverer; each of them would be a stimulus and a challenge to the other. Gisela watched him from the mirror, and the warm, heavy, lingering smile of her love played upon him without concealment. She thought he was safely clear of all his doubts and reservations concerning the death of Marc Chatrier; but suddenly the shadow was back in his eyes, and he harked back to it again, as it seemed she must be prepared for him to do many times yet before the place in his mind healed.

" One thing bothers me," said Johnny. " Codger never thought of that by himself, you know—either time. He never hurt anybody in his life off his own bat, only when he was told. Someone told him to do it. And I'm horribly afraid it was me. I know I said something about knocking off Musgrave—you remember?"

" But he'd often heard things like that said, and never taken them seriously."

" But that time I meant it. I did mean it! Only for
a minute, but . . . From other people he had to have
orders spelled out, but from me a hint was enough. He
might have sensed that I was in dead earnest—I wish
to God I knew! "

" You were *not*," she said quickly and fiercely.

" Then he must have thought I was. Damn it, I
don't know myself. And something comes back to me
now about the other time, about Chatrier. I said something about him, too, a day or so before it happened.
Something about him being due for a funeral, not a
wedding, if everybody had his deserts. I didn't say it
to Codger—but Codger was there. Gisela, Codger only
did what he thought I wanted! In the end I'm to
blame."

" Oh, Johnny! " she said, and turned suddenly and
took his face between her hands. " Oh, Johnny;
oh, my darling, don't! I love you, and I can't bear
any more. Let it alone, let it alone, and don't kill
me! "

She got him to the bottom of the stairs safely, silent
and dazed between the revelations of his wretchedness
and his happiness. They were very late. The theatre
was hushed and still, but its emptiness felt warm and
at ease, without a qualm for dead Figaro. In Sam's box
by the stage-door there was an ache where Codger had
been, but even there, it seemed, there could be no
permanent void. Sam's voice, gruff and querulous,
addressed some unseen presence within:

" Take your tail out o' that fire, you daft mutt, and
get from underfoot."

The dog Buster, a stray with one wall eye, had

walked in and insinuated himself into Sam's room yesterday morning, draggled with rain. Not an attractive beast, nor a bright one, but bright enough to recognise encouragement beneath what had sounded like the opposite. Probably Sam wouldn't have welcomed a more presentable specimen. The vacancy wouldn't have fitted anything but a helpless, well-meaning creature doomed eternally to be a liability and a nuisance.

In the corridor Johnny halted abruptly.

"Wait a minute!" he said, labouring with a new thought. "New blue plastic knitting-needles! He had those the night before the murder, I remember seeing them when he showed me the sweater he was knitting for Hans. Who gave him those? Codger couldn't shop for the simplest thing, that was one thing Dolly never left to him. Someone provided him with those needles —*before he killed Chatrier*."

"Johnny, let it rest."

"I can't. Somebody planned it, somebody made use of him. It wasn't just that I said something that set him off—because somebody acted, somebody gave him the new needles and took the old ones . . ."

Sam had heard their voices, low as they were, and emerged from his box, the dog at his heels. He seemed to have shrunk since he had lost Codger, the big frame hung lank inside his clothes, the lines of his face were fallen into a mournful mask.

"I thought you'd decided to stay the night," he said. "Tom's been kicking his heels outside twenty minutes, waiting for you."

Johnny seemed not to have heard a word of this. He stood staring at the old man with the flare of a wild suspicion in his eyes, and fought to bring the point-blank question out of his throat, where it was stuck fast and choking him.

" Sam, tell me something. And tell me the truth. Did *you* put Codger up to killing Chatrier? "

They looked at each other for a moment in silence, the shock almost palpable on the air between them. Sam's ancient eyes, that had seen Johnny grow from an insubordinate cadet to the man he was now, and never underestimated him and never gone in awe of him, fixed him with a steely gleam of indignation that could not quite burn into anger.

" No," he said, " I did not. What do you think I am? Me, that's looked after the poor beggar like a nursemaid all these years? No, I didn't. And if you ever ask me a thing like that again, so help me, Johnny Truscott, I'll clout you."

Johnny knew the truth when he heard and saw it, at least in Sam. He heaved the horrible doubt off his chest in a gasping sigh of relief.

" So help me, you should have done it this time," he said. " I beg your pardon, Sam. I ought to have known better."

And indeed he ought. Who had been more constant in his care for the poor wreck the sea had left of Codger? The night he'd mislaid his charge he'd had Martin out helping him to scour the neighbourhood, frantic with anxiety, until Johnny had telephoned from the police station to break the news to him. Without his burden he'd lost the obstinate energy that had been the mainspring of his life. Johnny saw suddenly and piteously how old he was, how the hard flesh had begun to dry up on his bones. What sort of friend was it who couldn't do him the bare justice he himself had received from Musgrave?

"That's all right, lad. We're all a bit out of ourselves. Get on home to bed, and forget it."

He saw them out to the top of the steps, and the car was waiting below in a dim, desultory haze of rain. The long-legged dog pressed close at Sam's heels, leaning against his twisted knee; it had chosen its place, and did not intend to be dislodged.

"Don't come down, Sam," said Gisela. "You go back inside, out of the rain."

"All right, if you say so. Good night, miss!" He dug a hard fist into Johnny's ribs, administering painful comfort. "'Night, Johnny!"

"Good night, Sam," said Johnny, shivering with unreasonable shame, and went down the steps to the car confused and sad and resigned and hopeful all at once, with Gisela in his arm.

"All the same, *someone*——" he said.

"No, not necessarily. What do we know about the country of his mind, Johnny? We're all without maps, there. Maybe he understood more than we knew, maybe he could do much more than we thought— when it was for you. Let him rest, Johnny," she said in his ear. "Stop now. There's a time to stop, for everybody's sake." Her cheek stooped briefly to his shoulder in a muted caress that made his heart lurch in him. "Stop before you break things," she said.

She felt then that his will to resist her was being lulled to sleep, that she was the certainty and the comfort in the chaos of his mind, and that she had only to remain close beside him and his hopeless inward inquiries would cease. Already the urgency was ebbing out of him, the tension slackening out of his tired body and troubled spirit. Let it alone now. Let him rest.

They had reached the bottom of the steps when she said suddenly: " Oh, wait a moment for me, please, I shall have to go back. I left a letter behind. . . . Sam told me there was one by the late delivery, and I never collected it. He must have forgotten it, too. I won't be a moment."

" I'll go," said Johnny.

" No, you wait for me. I'll only be a moment." And she ran back up the steps before he could insist, and vanished through the swinging door.

Sam had been scraping out the bowl of his foul old pipe with a penknife worn down to a sliver of steel, and was testing the result without much optimism. He blew, and the stem bubbled like a boiling kettle; he sucked, and drew distressing noises from it, like a cow proceeding with ponderous deliberation through a swamp. A bit of dottle, disturbed by the knife, had lodged deep in the bottom of the bowl. He couldn't displace it with the blade; he stretched one hand to his table drawer, rummaged in it blindly, and prodded discontentedly in the bottom of the offending briar with the first implement that came to hand. It wasn't much good for the job, too long and too thick, but he persevered obstinately. The point grated sadly in the charged wood, the rounded knob wagged by Sam's right ear.

A voice from the doorway said quietly: " Sam! "

He dropped his unwieldy tool into the drawer, and shut it to with a quick but calm movement, and turned

to face Gisela. She had come in so silently that even the
dog had done no more than elevate one shaggy ear and
open one disconcerting white eye. She closed the door
gently behind her, and stood leaning against it, her
dark eyes wide and still.

Sam got to his feet with the rocking motion peculiar
to his maimed legs, and the dog, stretched out at his
feet, kept its chin possessively across his toes and cocked
a wild eye at Gisela. Sam's eyes had never been more
tranquil. He looked at her without a smile, thoughtfully, almost expectantly, and said mildly: " Forget
something, miss ? "

" Yes, Sam. A letter, for Johnny's benefit. And for
yours, just something I had to say."

She left the door and came forward a few steps into
the room, her gaze steady and kind and sad upon his
face.

" Simply that you needn't worry. Johnny'll be all
right, I'll take care of Johnny. He'll never know anything more from me than he knows now."

He looked back at her uncomprehendingly, with
eyes blank as pebbles, as though she had spoken to him
in a foreign language; but she caught some communication that came from deeper within and needed no
visible expression, for she smiled wanly, and answered
what he would not ask.

" No, *I* didn't lie to him, either. Like you, I didn't
have to. There was no need for me to tell him *who* it
was I saw in the wings that night. *He* told *me*. He
made it easy for both of us. And that's the way it must
stay, Sam, for Johnny's sake. He's lost one man he
was fond of, he shan't lose two. Not for a Marc
Chatrier."

The old man's eyes, opaque and still, watched her and made no acknowledgement.

" It was wickedly foolish," she said, a tremor shaking her voice for an instant, " to use a weapon that pointed so obviously to Codger—when he was close at hand there, and sure to be suspected. But who am I to talk? I did worse than that to him when he was dead. And I did it knowingly, with intent. I thought he wouldn't grudge it, for Johnny. Or for you."

He shook his head slightly, and continued mute. What was there to say that wouldn't be better left unsaid? She was the one who knew how to put things. Some day she'd even get around to working out how carefully he'd installed Codger upstairs with Dolly, and how sick he'd felt when he'd seen him there in the wings, and realised that the poor old fool had slipped off after him, and left his nice, safe alibi behind him. No need to tell her; when she thought a bit, she'd know.

" But you can't foresee everything," said Gisela sadly, as though she had followed the mournful trajectory of his thoughts. " We're all so tangled up together, guilty and innocent, there's no point now in trying to sort it out. Codger's dead, and the act that killed him was at least his own act. Maybe that half absolves the rest of us. God knows! "

" I dare say you're right, miss," said Sam, like an old man humouring a child whose chatter he has not even heard properly, much less troubled to understand.

" So good night, Sam, and don't worry."

In the doorway she checked again for an instant, and looked back. " Oh, and Sam——"

" Yes, miss? "

Her dark eyes lingered for a moment upon the table drawer. She looked up into the old man's face, and the veil of isolation was drawn back from between them for one blinding instant before she turned her eyes away.

" Get rid of it, Sam," she said, rapid and low. " Now, before Martin comes on duty. I'll buy you some proper pipe-cleaners to-morrow."

She was gone. He heard the outer door swing after her, and her light steps running down in haste to Johnny; and in a moment the car purred away round the forecourt and out on to the road.

Sam pulled the drawer open, and took up with blunt brown fingers the solitary steel knitting-needle that lay among the litter of small things within. She was right, of course, it would have to go. He wondered what they would do with the other one, or what they had already done with it. Something safe and final.

He took his foot, not too brusquely, from under the dog's reluctant and protesting chin; and Buster, heaving himself out of his half-sleep with a gusty sigh, followed his lame god down to the furnace.

THE END